LORD HAVE MERCY,
EXCEPT FOR . . .

Slocum set down the shovel, took off his hat, and spoke over the woman's grave.

"Lord," he said, looking upward, "this here's Mrs. Tyler, who was took in childbirth. I believe she was a good woman, 'cause she got the cord cut and the baby covered while she knew she was dyin' herself.

"Well, tell her I'm gonna do right by him, as right as she did. She was a good mama for what little time she had, and I hope she'll be a good angel to you, Lord. Amen."

He started to put on his hat, then paused.

"Lord?" he added. "If you can find that good-for-nothin' husband that run off and left her in such terrible straits, I'd greatly appreciate it if you could give him a good kick in the ass. Amen for true, this time."

JAKE LOGAN

SLOCUM
AND THE ORPHAN EXPRESS

JOVE BOOKS, NEW YORK

SLOCUM AND THE ORPHAN EXPRESS

A Jove Book / published by arrangement with
the author

PRINTING HISTORY
Jove edition / May 2004

ISBN: 0-515-13733-2

A JOVE BOOK®
Jove Books are published by The Berkley Publishing Group,
a division of Penguin Group (USA) Inc.,
375 Hudson Street, New York, New York 10014.
JOVE and the "J" design
are trademarks belonging to Penguin Group (USA) Inc.

PRINTED IN THE UNITED STATES OF AMERICA

10 9 8 7 6 5 4 3 2 1

1

It was a particularly nasty patch of the Arizona Territory that Slocum was riding through.

He hadn't seen a living soul for four days, and not a drop of fresh water for three. All he had for company—besides his Appaloosa gelding, Tubac—was a wind that for two days had been threatening to turn into a full-fledged, hang-on-to-your-hat-and-britches, can't-breathe-nor-see-worth-shit dust storm, but had so far been content—in this location, at least—to just annoy the holy hell out of him.

It clogged his food, got in his eyes, stung his cheeks, made it nigh on impossible to see more than about twenty feet most of the time, and it was really beginning to piss him off.

Of course, he didn't have much else to be mad at except the weather. For a change.

He'd just finished making the rounds of bounty collecting for a little job he'd taken on over New Mexico way. Despite having given some of the cash to a couple of down-on-their luck farmers, and some more of it to a pretty little whore who didn't want to be a whore anymore, he was a fairly wealthy man.

He'd spent some time up in Prescott. He'd kicked up a storm on Whiskey Row and had himself a high old champagne-drinking and Cuban cigar–smoking time—not to mention one sloe-eyed, extremely sultry, half-Mexican, half-French little smoker of a tart named Cabochon Lolita Gomez. And he hadn't run into one blessed soul who wanted to shoot him.

That was one for the record books, right there.

Plus, he managed to hang on to over seven thousand in cash, most of which was sewn into the lining of his clothes.

Slocum might have a deceptively devil-may-care attitude toward the ladies and the booze and those cherished Havana cigars, but there were three specific things he took dead serious: his horse, his guns, and his money.

He was just thinking that maybe the storm was finally going to rise up and blow full force. Grit was beginning to do more than sting his face—what part of it that wasn't covered by his raised bandana—and visibility had dropped to about ten feet.

He squinted into the wind, trying to locate some kind of shelter. There had been some big red rocks in the distance a while back when the wind took a break. But he couldn't see a damned thing.

He dropped his reins, and shouted through the escalating blow, "You find it, Tubac. I can't see worth shit."

The loud-colored leopard Appy—whose nose Slocum had loosely rigged over with a bandana that morning—may have looked pretty silly, but at least he could breathe. And it seemed he could almost smell those rocks, too.

Once Slocum gave him his head, he started off at an angle, head down. Slocum was just content to sit there, and finally, about ten minutes later, he practically walked straight into those red rocks.

They weren't much, just some jagged sandstone pillars about twelve or fourteen high. They rose out of the flat surroundings like a old dog's molars jut from his battered gums.

Slocum was mighty glad to see them, though.

He picked up his reins again, and reined Tubac back inside. There was quite a stand of the ancient stones, some jagged, some rounded, and the wind whistled through them like the sounds of murdered Apache ghosts. But it was shelter.

And Slocum wasn't the sort to be superstitious.

He got down off Tubac, and shouted, "Good boy! Now let's see if we can't find us a nice corner to get tucked into for the duration!" He led the horse around the rocks, weaving and backtracking and feeling his way along until he found just the right place.

With no more wind lashing at his back, he stripped the tack—and the bandana—off Tubac, and led him close to a big, curved rock, where he was out of the blow. Or at least, most of him was.

Slocum watered him, although not as much as he would have wished. He was down to parceling out water until he found a new source.

"Gonna have to do for now, boy," he said over the wind howling through the rocks. He ran his hand down the gelding's once-snowy neck, and saw it come away gritty and dark.

Shaking his head in disgust, he added, "I'll take the brushes to you after I get myself some grub."

Strapping on Tubac's feed bag, the wind whistling and crying through his ears, he thought better of the brushing. "Hell, I'll wait till tomorrow, old son. No sense in doin' it all over again."

He squinted off into the howling wind, then patted the Appaloosa on his grimy neck. "Maybe this damned storm'll quiet down some by then."

• • •

When Slocum awoke the next morning, he thought the wind was still crying loud and strong.

Half-asleep and disappointed, he pulled off the bandana he'd tied over his lower face and pushed his hat off his upper face, only to discover that all was calm. The day had dawned crystal clear.

But why did he still hear the wind?

Tubac heard it, too. The gelding's head was turned toward an opening in the rocks, and his ears were pricked and alert.

"Sonofabitch!" Slocum muttered beneath his breath. He quietly stood up, feeling old injuries slither grumpily past the pain of waking and long-broken bones remembering their places. Unconsciously, he felt for his Colt and thumbed the strap off.

On foot, he started toward the sound.

He was past Tubac's rump before he realized what that wailing sound actually was: a baby. A human infant, crying.

Muttering, "What the...." he walked toward the sound, weaving his way between spires of rock as he tried to calculate its source. It wasn't easy with the sound bouncing off all that rock, but at last he wove his way through the maze of rock and to the other side of the ragged outcrop.

There, half-buried in sand, was a Conestoga wagon. It wasn't a long-bed, but it was still good-sized. There were no horses or oxen in sight, the traces were half buried in drifted sand, and it had a broken axle, which explained its being abandoned. Well, semi-abandoned. The wagon's canvas top was tattered but still more-or-less clinging to the ribs, and hung down from them limply, in seeming exhaustion. The rig looked to have been sitting there for a good, long time.

The baby was inside, although he couldn't see it, only hear it.

"Ma'am?" he called. If there was a baby, there had to be a mother.

But why was she out here, miles from nowhere? And furthermore, where was her husband?

There was no answer, so he shouted, "Ma'am!" again, this time adding, "Do you need help?"

Nothing but that bawling baby.

He stepped slowly up to the wagon, hoping that some jittery female wasn't in there, scared to death and ready to blast his head off with a Greener.

"I ain't gonna hurt you, ma'am," he said reassuringly as he closed the distance between himself and the nearest wagon wheel. "My name's Slocum. I've got some water here for you. Not much, but enough to share."

He put his boot on the step and pushed himself up, ready to leap back down at the first hint of a rifle's cock.

But none came. There was just that baby, crying and crying.

He climbed up onto the box and peered inside. "Hello?" he said.

There was a woman there, back in the shadows, but she wasn't moving.

Muttering, "Aw, shit," he scrambled inside the wagon and went to her.

She was dead and cold, there in the makeshift bed. She'd probably died sometime last night. And clutched in her lifeless and rigid arms was a newborn baby. It couldn't have been more than a couple days old, at the most. And there was pooled, partially congealed blood on the blankets.

Birthing blood.

He worked the baby from her cold arms. It had been wrapped in a white swaddling cloth, which he gently pulled away. The cord had been cut, all right, but his initial thought about the baby's age had been wrong. From the raw, fresh look of the cord, it must have been born last night.

Last night. He could have been there, if not for that damned wind cloaking the mother's presence. He would have heard something. He would have come.

But he hadn't heard. And he hadn't come.

And now the baby's mother, whoever she had been, was dead. She had been a pretty little thing, poor darling. Dark hair, poreless sun-browned skin, a high, clean brow. Her staring eyes were deep brown, the color of coffee, and still moist. He closed them with a gentle brush of his hand. She hadn't been dead more than a few hours.

He put the squalling baby down on a blanket at its mother's head, and began to hunt through their stores. Surely they had to have canned milk. It looked to him like they were on a long-haul trip.

And then he began to think, as he was going through the second makeshift cupboard, that if the mother had been out of water, she'd very possibly have drunk all the milk herself. Or maybe they hadn't had any need for canned milk in the first place. They might have had a cow that had taken off with their other livestock. And the husband.

Finally, his hand settled on one dusty can of Michaelson's Best Canned Evaporated Milk. It was the only one there was.

He pulled it free of tinned peaches and tinned beef. Then he dug out his pocketknife, punctured two holes in the lid, and turned toward the baby.

He had risen halfway out of his squat before he realized that the kid couldn't exactly hold up the can and gulp it down.

"Aw, hell," he said. He made no attempt to keep his voice down. The baby couldn't hear him over its own wails, anyway.

He looked around the wagon, peering under blankets

and tarps, digging through boxes and crates. He found a framed wedding picture of the mother and a thin, tall, blond man. On the back it read, *Mr. and Mrs. Justin Tyler* in a spidery, handwritten script, but that was all. No date. No first name for her. Only the stamp *Fairfield Photography* at the bottom. It didn't even say if Fairfield was the name of a town or the name of the photographer.

At last, he found sort of a boxed kit that had been made up for the baby, likely weeks or months before. In it, he found a few tiny homemade clothes, knitted booties and such, a slim stack of white diapers, some pins, talcum powder, lanolin and other potions, oils, lotions, and remedies.

And along with them, a couple of small bottles, complete with rubber nipples.

"Thank God," he said as he poured a little of the milk into one of the bottles, then capped it carefully with a nipple. "You were sure prepared for just about everything, weren't you, Mrs. Tyler?" he asked the still mother.

"All right, all right," he soothed as he picked up the baby again. He pushed the nipple against its red lips. "Just a little for now. Wish you could tell me where your daddy went."

Luckily for Slocum, the baby took the nipple right away and nursed greedily. "The next one'll have to be water, kid," he said. "It's three days' ride east to Cross Point, and that's without holding a baby in my lap. How do you feel about horses?"

To the sounds of the baby's suckling, he looked around the wagon, deciding what could be taken along, and what would have to be retrieved later. That baby kit, he'd take that for sure. He just wished there'd been more canned milk.

He decided to grab a can of tinned peaches, for himself. He didn't think they'd mind, and he could use something sweet.

He'd take the picture of the kid's parents, too. Maybe somebody over in Cross Point could identify them, if they'd come through there on their way west.

And then he realized that he didn't even know if the kid was a he or a she. He waited until the baby finished nursing, then peeled back the swaddling cloth. He was greeted by a stink that had him blinking and holding his breath, but at least he knew the sex of the child.

"Well, young Master Tyler," he said, squinting against the smell as he lay the child down again, "let me go get my gear, and then we'll see to your mama, here. And to that diaper."

Slocum set down the shovel he'd found in the Tylers' wagon, took off his hat, and wiped his brow on his sleeve before he took up what he hoped was a reverent posture at the side of the grave he'd just covered.

"Lord," he said, looking upward, toward the heavens, "this here's Mrs. Tyler, who was took in childbirth. I believe she was a good woman, 'cause she got the cord cut and the baby covered even while she was bleedin' to death."

He studied the baby. "Wouldn't be surprised but what she nursed him as best she could, too. Tell her I'm gonna do right by him, as right as she did. She was a good mama for what little time she had, and I hope she'll be a good angel to you, Lord. Amen."

He started to put on his hat, then paused. "Lord?" he added. "If you can find that good-for-nothin' husband that run off and left her in such terrible straits, I'd appreciate it if you could give him a good kick in the ass. Amen for true, this time."

He settled his hat firmly on his head.

"Well," he said to the baby, "reckon I've done all I can, kid. 'Cept for this." He bent over and picked up a wide stake he'd made from a board on the wagon's gate, and upon which he'd painted the legend, *Mrs. Justin Tyler*.

He thrust it into the ground at the grave's head, then gave it a couple of whacks with the shovel, just to make sure it was in good and firm. He wondered how long the words would last, seeing as how he'd written them in a watery whitewash that they'd apparently used on the wagon from time to time.

He supposed that if it didn't rain much—out here, it might not rain for months and months—it'd probably stay painted long enough for somebody over in Cross Point to haul a real marker out here for her grave.

That was, if Cross Point was still a town in thriving operation. He hadn't been there in a long spell.

"I got everything packed up, kid," he said, even though the baby certainly couldn't understand him. "Got your little case and the rest of that can a' milk. Damned if I'm takin' those dirty britches you was wrapped up in, though."

He snugged Tubac's cinch and once again checked the packs he'd tied behind his saddle, and the extra water bag. Mrs. Tyler hadn't been out of water, after all. She'd had nearly a full bag.

Shaking his head, he patted Tubac's chestnut and white neck. "Damn shame," he muttered to the horse before he picked up the baby. He'd cleaned the child up the best he could, and then diapered him and wrapped him in one of Mrs. Tyler's spare petticoats. It was nice and clean, and Slocum didn't think she would have cared.

The child in his arms, he carefully swung up into the saddle. The baby didn't cry. That was a good sign, he thought hopefully.

"See?" Slocum said to the tiny boy with the tiny and very serious face. The kid reminded him a little of his grampa, mainly because he was so wrinkled and pruny.

Well, that would pass, he reckoned. He just wasn't sure when.

"We're gonna take us a ride on this nice big horse," he said, being of the opinion that babies were a little like cows. They didn't fuss too much if you just kept on talking or singing to them. And he sure as hell wasn't going to sing.

He reined Tubac around and headed him east, toward Cross Point.

2

When Lydia West awoke that morning, the wind had stopped. Slowly, she crawled from under her blanket and out of the little hollow in which she'd taken shelter, not believing that such a miracle could have happened.

But it had.

The desert was still, the sky was clear. There was a light, teasing breeze, but that was all. The only thing that betrayed the former presence of that blinding, endless, screeching wind was a coating of fine, powdery dust on everything—including her.

She walked toward a low shrub and gave it a half-hearted kick. Dust shivered down from its leaves to the ground.

"Winston?" she said to no one in particular. There was no one else there. "I can see clear across this goddamn valley."

And it was endless, or so it seemed. How many miles until she reached those low mountains in the distance? There was hardly a bush or tree or even cactus of any consequence in sight.

Lydia frowned, sighing, and then began to pick up the few possessions she had with her. The few possessions

11

she had in the world, she reminded herself.

She assembled them in her shawl, which she had patched several times over the last few days, and made a secure pouch, which she tied to her waist.

She shook out her once emerald-green skirts the best she could, although it didn't matter. Nothing really mattered anymore, did it?

She didn't have enough water to make it to Cross Point, unless she lucked across a tank or a spring. She didn't even have enough to make it much past sundown.

And even if she managed to get back to civilization, what then? She'd have to tell the sheriff, and pretty soon the whole town would know that Winston had been a fool and that she was, too.

And a sullied one at that. Not that she wasn't sullied to start with.

"Damn you, Winston," she muttered.

Then, tying her scarf over her head and pulling it forward to shade her face from the merciless sun, she set off toward the east.

For some reason, Lydia had been thinking that if only the wind would let up, if only she could see more than a few feet, she'd make better time. She didn't, though. The wind and the dark clouds had at least kept the sun from her, and today was clear and hot. Beastly hot.

She had to stop by ten in the morning and huddle in the meager shade of a small pile of rocks, making herself sip carefully at her dwindling supply of water.

Before, it had seemed almost magically easy. Winston had married her, right out of the clear blue sky, and taken her away from Madame Trudy's up in Flagstaff. She'd never really loved Winston, not in the all-out, romantic way. However, she'd surely been grateful to him for taking her away from Trudy's viselike financial grip, and vowed to make him the best wife that she could.

Hell, she just couldn't get ahead at Trudy's, what with the charges for laundry, charges for the room, charges for meals, charges for this and that.

She wasn't a shirker. Far from it. But at the end of each week all she'd have left for her toil beneath ranchers and cowboys and miners and passers-through was about a quarter.

If she was lucky.

So when Winston West came along—and then came back again and again and again, the last time with a ring in his pocket—she wasn't about to tell him no.

They had moved south, where nobody knew her. Well, at the time, she'd thought that Winston had done it for her. Winston put his savings into a little ranch and some livestock, and they'd been fairly happy. That was, until she found out.

Found out about Winston, that was. It turned out that he wasn't a Colorado rancher's pleasant-faced second son after all. Neither was he a Baptist, nor did he have an income from back home, nor was he single. And his name wasn't even Winston West.

Now, Linda could have forgiven any of those things. She could, in fact, have forgiven them all. She wasn't so pure herself, was she? But at least she'd come into the marriage with all her truths hanging out in plain sight, so to speak.

Winston, the sonofabitch, had been a big pack of lies right from the beginning. And a married pack of lies, to boot!

She'd found out everything all at once, last week, when Billy Cree and his gang rode into her ranch yard and shot Winston dead, right there by the stock tank. He didn't even have time to put his bucket down, let alone run for his rifle.

Billy Cree and his boys, Randy and Wes, had finished off the day—and the following night and morning—by raping her. It was highly unpleasant, to say the least, but at least they didn't kill her right off. And when at last they were done with her and gathered in the parlor, arguing over whether to kill her or not, she'd pulled down Winston's spare Colt pistol and her old .22 derringer, and shot all three of them from the open bedroom door, just like fish in a barrel.

The last one to go—Wes, she thought it was—had time to draw his pistol and get a shot off, but it wasn't any good. She imagined it had lodged somewhere in her parlor wall.

Even after they were dead, they had all looked so surprised.

The bastards.

She supposed she'd sat there for hours, just staring at the bodies, fallen atop each other like so much kindling, before she got the strength—and the energy—to do something.

She and Winston had lived far from the nearest town, Override, and Override wasn't there anymore. It had closed its last door and banged its last shutter about a year earlier when the silver vein south of town petered out. The other ranchers—all three of them—had pulled up stakes and gone too, leaving them the only living souls within a forty-mile radius.

She should have known right then that Winston wasn't on the up and up. She remembered thinking, Who the hell would want to ranch so far from anything remotely resembling civilization?

Lydia knew she had to go somewhere, but Override wasn't it. The nearest inhabited place was Bethel, but that was across the high mountain range to the west, and she didn't think she was up to that.

Cross Point was in the opposite direction, and she'd have to cross some low hills, but she decided it was her best option.

Cross Point it would be, then.

She'd stood up and washed herself double-hard and put on some clothes, and then she went out into the yard, where Winston's crow- and vulture-picked body had been lying since yesterday afternoon.

While, one by one, she hauled and tugged and carried rocks to cover the body good enough so that the coyotes couldn't get to it, she vaguely wondered whether she should put Winston Q. West on the marker, or his other name, as spoken by Billy Cree and his buddies: the Show Low Kid.

In the end, she left him no marker at all.

She'd packed up enough water and food to make the journey, thrown in several small personal things she didn't want the desert to have, and turned out all the livestock—what there was up by the house, anyway—except her riding horse. She shooed away the outlaws' horses, saw them canter off into the distance. The next morning, she left.

She had abandoned the outlaws' bodies in the house and left the door wide open, as an invitation to coyotes and other vermin. She had no intention of returning. And she didn't much care what happened to Cree and his friends' earthly remains, although she halfway hoped it was reasonably gruesome.

Now it was four days later. More like four days of hell.

She'd run straight into a windstorm that she thought would never cease, lost Winston's poor old horse to a big, fat diamondback rattler, and lost half her supplies, too. And at the moment, she was sitting hunkered in the pathetic shade of those rocks and beginning to wonder, quite seriously, if she'd get out of this alive at all.

She supposed most people would have asked themselves that question about four days ago, when the wind was just beginning to howl up a storm and that dad-gum snake bit her horse.

Not her, though.

Despite everything that had happened to her in her twenty-six short years, Lydia West was still an optimist at heart. Somehow, she always expected that things would be looking up any minute.

Well, sometimes they did and sometimes they didn't.

And right now was beginning to look like one of those "didn't" times.

She sighed, and wearily hoisted herself up to her feet.

"Damn you, Winston," she muttered, and started out toward the east again.

Slocum dropped his reins and let Tubac walk along beneath him. The kid was crying again, which had interrupted an awful nice daydream about Cindy-May Cummings and her sisters, Annie and Pitty-Pat. They had all three set upon him one night, up in Prescott, and they had shown him a time he'd never forget as long as he lived.

One sucked his cock while another kissed his mouth and rubbed her titties against him, while another one nibbled his ears and talked dirty to him and . . . other things.

Why, there were practically as many titties to grab at as there were on a nursing barn cat. And a whole lot riper and nicer, too!

But then, all those nice and nasty thoughts went *whoosh* when the baby started crying.

Slocum supposed he couldn't blame him. Only about a day old, if that, and this kid had seen more crud than most men see in five years.

Reluctantly leaving behind thoughts about Pitty-Pat and Annie and Cindy-May, Slocum fished the little bottle from his pocket and carefully tried to pour in water from his canteen without dropping the kid or the bottle. Or the canteen.

He finally succeeded, and slipped the nipple onto the bottle. He wagged it at the baby, who just kept on crying.

"Damn it, kid, take it," he muttered, gently forcing the nipple between the baby's lips.

After a moment, the baby began to suck.

He didn't look real pleased about the offering, though.

"Sorry," Slocum said. "Your milk's in my saddlebags, what there is of it. You're gonna have to go slow on the white stuff, or you'll run out. Ain't no cows or goats out here. No general stores, either."

The baby kept sucking lackadaisically at the bottle and ignoring Slocum.

"Well, as long as you ain't cryin'. . . ." Slocum mumbled, steadying the baby in the crook of his arm. The kid had a shock of fine, silky, setter-red hair, and brown eyes with sorrel lashes that halfway covered his cheeks when he slept.

Which hadn't been a hell of a lot.

"I'm tired of tellin' you stories, junior," Slocum went on. "You mind if I shut up for a while?"

The baby gave no sign, so he figured the kid didn't much mind one way or the other.

Good, because Slocum was working on a sore throat. Hell, he hadn't talked so much right straight in a row since the time he was down in Mexico with Tad Thurnston about five years back. Thurnston had gotten himself a concussion from Birdy Ramirez cracking him over the head with a tequila bottle, and Slocum had to talk to him all night to keep him awake.

Course, Thurnston up and died two days later when Birdy Ramirez snuck in the shack and nailed him with a .45, which then demanded that Slocum go out and ride Birdy down and plug him for Thurnston—but that was beside the point.

The kid finished his bottle and spat out the nipple with a little bubble. Slocum was all set for him to start bawling again, but he didn't. Instead, he yawned wide and sort of twisted and scrunched his little old man's face around, closed his eyes, and went right to sleep.

Careful not to disturb him, Slocum tucked the bottle back into his pocket.

Good old Tubac had kept up a slow and steady pace in just the right direction all during the feeding, and Slocum supposed there wasn't much point in it, but he picked up the reins anyway.

And then, quite suddenly, he was glad that he had.

"Whoa, son," he said softly as he reined Tubac to a halt.

He twisted, reaching back toward his saddlebag. Fishing out his spyglass, he hooked the top lip of it on the lip of his saddle skirts and pulled it open. He raised it to his eye.

"Jesus." He breathed as he squinted through the lenses. "A woman? What the hell's a woman doin' out here? And on foot!"

Then again, what was that other woman doing out here having a baby all by her lonesome?

It was turning from a real strange day into a truly remarkable one.

Smacking the spyglass on his thigh to close it, he stuck it back down into his saddlebag, and reined Tubac south, toward the solitary moving speck that he knew was a woman in a green dress.

He couldn't tell much more than that from this distance, but she was a woman all right, and she was alone.

Hell, she'd probably be as glad to see him as he'd been to see her.

After all, old or young, ugly or fair, she was a woman, wasn't she? She'd have to know something about babies.

3

At first, Lydia thought that the shape approaching through a shimmer of desert heat was a lost, lone pronghorn. Nothing to be afraid of.

But as it neared, she realized that it was a horse, and that it was mounted.

There was nowhere to take cover, nowhere to run, and he was loping right down on her.

She crouched down, feverishly hunting through her makeshift bag for Winston's spare Colt, the one she'd shot Billy Cree and his buddies with. In her other hand, she held the little .22 derringer.

She would not be raped again, by God. She wouldn't suffer that. She'd kill the sonofabitch before he had a chance to touch her.

Her fingers found the Colt's butt-end just as the rider slowed to a trot. By the time he had slowed to a walk, she freed it and held it out at arm's length, pointed directly at his heart.

Or so she hoped.

"Stop right there!" she shouted to him.

The rider, who seemed to be cradling a bundle of rags for some odd reason, reined in his horse, quickly looped the reins over his saddle horn, then waved his free hand.

"Don't mean you no harm, ma'am!" he shouted. "It's just that I got this—"

"You can turn right around and leave the way you came," she shouted back. The effort made her dry, scratchy throat hurt. "But drop your water," she added quickly.

She reasoned that it was only fair that she got something out of this.

The cowboy let a water bag slide from his saddle to the ground with a damp and sloshy *plop*. It looked about half-full, which was dandy with her. She'd make it to Cross Point just fine, thank you.

"Look, lady," the cowboy began.

But she cut him off with a wave of Winston's pistol and a shouted, "Now, go on! Get out of here!"

"You're not—" the cowboy began again, and this time she stopped him by raising the derringer, too, and firing a shot into the air.

The sound startled even her, but the cowhand's horse did nothing more than lift its muzzle a tad and cock its ears. And before she had time to fully take in how very odd that was, a baby started crying.

A baby?

The cowboy looked down at the bundle in his arm and started talking to it softly. She couldn't make out the words.

She knew that the bundle of rags was a baby, though. She hadn't made it up in her head. The sun hadn't baked her that nutty, not yet.

"Get down off your horse," she called, before she thought about it. And as he carefully dismounted, she realized what a stupid thing that had been, asking him to climb down even if he did have a child with him.

A man could still lay aside a child and rape her, couldn't he?

A man could just as easily lay that child aside and kill her.

Hell, he wouldn't even have to shift the kid to do it. He could reach for his gun one-handed, couldn't he? And his right hand was free.

He began to walk toward her.

"One hand in the air, if you don't mind," she called out in a rasp.

He complied, although he looked a tad grouchy about it. Actually, as he came closer, she decided that if the circumstances had been different, she would have thought him a very interesting looking man. Not handsome in a classical sense, but ruggedly so, as if he'd been around and seen some things in his time. It was a look she liked on a man.

He was tall and dark-haired and well-built, and when he walked up to her and stopped, she saw that he was green-eyed.

He didn't look like a rapist.

But then, you could never be too careful.

"Mind if I hoist this kid with both hands, lady?" he asked over the child's squall. There was something about his eyes that told her he wasn't taking her very seriously, even though by this time, she was aiming two guns at him. She thought that he seemed actually amused by her!

I'll show you amusing, you sonofabitch, she thought and waved the Colt's nose again.

"Where'd you come by that poor little child?" she demanded over the sound of the baby's crying. "Is she yours?"

"It's a 'him', and I found him back a few miles," the cowboy said, indicating the direction with a nod of his clean-shaven jaw. "I was too late to save his mama, but I buried her and brought him along. Don't figure he's even a day old, yet."

He held the child toward her, but Lydia wasn't that

stupid. She backed up a step, keeping Winston's gun and the derringer aimed at his chest—what part of it wasn't covered by the baby—and said, "Not so fast, mister."

"The name's Slocum, ma'am," he replied—quite civilly, considering she had two guns aimed at him. Then he peered down into the mewling, squalling bundle cradled in the crook of his arm and said, "Jesus, kid, cut me a little slack, will you?"

She just stared at him.

He looked up again, right into her eyes, and said, "Look, lady, I know you ain't got a reason in the world to trust me. But you look to be as much a dog in the manger as I feel like. I mean, you bein' out here with no horse and all. Me? I'm stuck with this baby. Only found one tin of milk in the wagon, and he keeps on cryin' all the damned time. Why, he's only slept about an hour altogether since we started out. I figured, you being a woman and all . . ."

Now, how on God's green earth did men come to conclusions like that? Just because she had the equipment to produce children didn't mean she knew the slightest thing about them!

"That I'd know something about babies?" she finished, brows lifted.

Oblivious to the sarcasm, Slocum nodded gravely. "That's about the size of it. When I spied you, I figured maybe the Lord was on this little feller's side after all."

Lydia considered this. Slocum certainly looked sincere. She'd thought at first that perhaps he'd killed the child's parents. But then, why hadn't he killed the child, too, if that were so?

Maybe he was just what he looked like: a saddle tramp—a good-looking saddle tramp—who had happened across a baby and come to its rescue.

She decided to take a chance.

She lowered both guns and let herself relax. A little.

"Well, I don't know anything about babies, either," she said, her voice cracking. Suddenly, her legs wobbled beneath her, and she sank down to the ground, thinking that perhaps she had let herself relax too much, and now it was too late to stop.

Fortunately, Slocum made no move that even she could term aggressive. He knelt down next to her, freed up a hand and felt her forehead.

"You could use some water, lady," he said, his brow furrowing with concern. "How long you been out here, anyway?"

"Days," she said. "Four, I think. I don't know."

"You got a name?"

"Lydia," she replied. "Lydia West." Maybe she should have said "Mrs. Show Low Kid," but that would have taken too long to explain, and she didn't feel much like talking right at the moment.

Besides, it required too much energy to be heard over the baby.

Slocum whistled, and his horse started toward him at a trot. Neat trick, she thought. The horse stopped beside him and pushed at him with its nose.

"Okay, Tubac, okay," he said. Gently, he handed over the baby. "Here," he said. "You hold on to him for a while."

And then he looked down at his shirt, which was damp with baby pee.

"Aw, crud," he said, and pulled down his canteen.

Charlie Frame kicked at one of the wagon wheels.

"Damn!" He breathed. "Hellfire and damnation!"

Somebody had come along, all right, because Mrs. Tyler sure hadn't up and buried herself. He wondered if she'd had the kid, and if it had survived. He sure hoped so, although that was sort of fighting the odds. Ed said he was always fighting the odds.

He was glad that Mrs. Tyler had kicked the bucket— she'd just saved him a bullet or two—but Jesus, he sure wished that baby of hers had made it through. It would have made things a whole lot easier.

When Justin Tyler had stumbled into his and Ed's camp a couple of nights before with the hell beaten out of him by the wind, Charlie and Ed had been right nice to him. Shared their hollow in the rocks, out of the wind, with old Justin and everything. Gave him coffee and grub, and pumped him for information.

Until you asked, you never could tell what stories a stranger had.

And you never could tell just what good a fellow might make of those stories for himself.

It turned out that Justin Tyler was chock-full of interesting tales. And that made Charlie and Ed real happy. Why, it seemed that Mister Justin Tyler was so nervous about his wife and his livestock that he just couldn't shut up once he got started.

Especially since he'd found such a nice couple of fellows to tell his story to.

Charlie and Ed had been a rapt audience.

This morning, when there was no wind anymore and they'd made short work of Mister Justin Tyler and left his body in that hollow in the rock, Charlie and Ed had set off the way Tyler said he'd come. They'd split up after an hour, though. There were no tracks left, and they figured they could cover more ground traveling separately.

Charlie hadn't seen hide nor hair of Ed since four hours past, although he'd passed what he figured was Tyler's milk cow. It was dead, and pretty chewed up by coyotes.

Didn't much matter, though. Mrs. Tyler was in the ground, as dead as her milk cow, and he sure as hell wasn't going to dig her up to see if that baby was buried with her or still in her belly.

Well, maybe he could salvage the situation. Maybe

there were things in the wagon worth taking. That deed had to be in there, didn't it? Tyler sure as hell hadn't had it on him.

Ed was going to be real disappointed, though, probably more disappointed than Charlie was right at this minute. Charlie could sure have used a gold mine out in California.

Well, half. When you counted Ed's half. And it would have been a whole lot easier if they'd turned up with that orphaned baby.

With a grunt, he hoisted himself up inside the wagon's bed.

He found dried, bloody rags all over the place. She'd had that baby, all right, by the looks of it. Made a bad job of it, too.

He cut as wide a berth as he could around the mess, and began to go through the Tylers' things. But he hadn't gone too far before he realized that somebody—probably the same somebody who'd buried Mrs. Tyler—had already ransacked the wagon, albeit neatly.

It wasn't too much longer before Charlie realized that there weren't any baby things in the wagon. No nappies, none of those little booties women liked to knit, no teeny tiny clothes. And there sure wasn't any deed to any gold mine.

"That kid's still alive," Charlie said out loud. "The kid's alive!"

Nobody would bother to take baby fixings if there wasn't a baby, would they? He didn't think so, not unless they were cracked in the head.

He went through the rest of the wagon quickly, tossing clothing and packed goods out the back end to the desert floor, looking for a piece of paper that wasn't there.

Swearing, he climbed down off the wagon and got back up on his bay horse. Whoever had that baby—and that deed—had to be headed toward Cross Point. Why, it was only a two-day ride—well, mayhap a three-day ride, if a man was having to carry a baby and had to travel easy—and the closest town in any direction.

He set out, following the fresh tracks in the now-still sand and gravel of the desert.

He'd told Ed he'd meet him in Cross Point, anyhow. This was going to work out just fine. 'Course, it'd be finer if he was to come across that helpful sonofabitch who'd buried Mrs. Tyler and saved her baby.

Charlie smiled and snapped his fingers, *pop!* That's what he'd like to do to that do-gooder. Charlie would teach that bastard to meddle in other people's business, and with other folks' gold mines.

Charlie'd teach him right good, that's what.

4

Slocum walked along beside Tubac. Lydia and the baby rode. He wasn't used to walking and didn't much like it, but it looked like he was stuck with traveling shank's mare, at least for the time being.

He had something to call the kid, now. That was the first thing Lydia had asked him once she'd hollered at him for not thinning the tinned milk, and for letting the baby stay wet for so long.

Well, hell! He didn't know!

'Course, she said she didn't know anything about babies either, but instinct was instinct. He kept the opinion to himself, though.

She sure was a tough little bird. He couldn't get much out of her, except that she was a rancher's wife whose man had died. She'd headed out for Cross Point, only to lose her saddle horse to a rattler several days back. By the way she acted, he figured there was quite a bit more to it than that, but once again, he kept his opinion to himself.

And the scenery was better with her along. She was tallish, maybe five-six or five-seven, and he suspected that underneath the desert grime she was real pretty. Her heart-shaped face held large, wide, blue-green eyes, a short, straight nose, and a ripe, pouty mouth, and was surrounded by yellow-gold hair the color of wheat ready to be harvested.

The figure was a nice one, too. Round, but not too round. Narrow in the right places and full where it mattered.

She was better looking than all three of those Cummings sisters put together. Even when you added in the half-Mexican, half-French whore to boot.

Right now she was cooing at the baby. "Who's a pretty baby, Tyler? Who's a handsome boy, baby Ty?"

Tyler. That's what she kept calling him. It was his folks' surname, after all, and she said that it was a fine first name, too, if a person didn't happen to have one. And now she'd already shortened it to Ty.

That baby hadn't cried once since she'd changed him. After he'd sucked down some of that watered milk, he'd slept for a while. But when he'd woken—and Slocum had cringed in expectation of an eardrum-shattering wail—he had only gurgled and blew bubbles and the like, and held on to Lydia's finger with a tiny, chubby fist.

She said it was because of the movement of the horse—the baby not crying, that was. Better than a rocking chair, she said.

Slocum was thinking that he'd had that kid up on top of Tubac, all morning, too, and that hadn't stopped him from bawling his fool little head off.

But Slocum wasn't going to say a word about it, no sir.

Besides, she was too downright pretty. He didn't want to get her riled up again.

He'd been walking for almost two hours, and he was ready for a stop. Actually, he'd been ready for it a good hour ago. Boots weren't made to walk in any farther than it took to jump off a horse and run to a roped calf—at least, not the kind that Slocum wore. And his leg muscles, which were used to gripping the sides of a horse, were about to kill him.

He stopped.

"What's wrong?" Lydia asked.

"Got to rest the horse," he lied.

She gave no indication that she'd seen through it, and asked, "Could you take Ty for a second so I can get down?"

"Sure," he said, and reached up to take the gurgling bundle.

Ty started crying again the moment he was in Slocum's arms.

"Shhh!" he hissed at the baby, who only bawled louder.

Lydia tried to hide a chuckle, but didn't quite succeed. She slid down from the saddle and held out her arms. "Here, let me have him again."

"He's all yours," replied Slocum, grateful to be rid of him.

And sure enough, the second little Ty felt himself in female arms again, he quieted right down.

Slocum thumbed back his hat and shook his head. "I'll be damned," he muttered.

Lydia smiled. "No, you won't, Mr. Slocum. Not by a long shot."

Slocum began to loosen Tubac's girth. "There's still a good bit of argument over that, Lydia. And knock off the 'Mister.' I keep thinking you're talkin' to my daddy. It's just Slocum."

She smiled, and sat down in the shade of the horse. "All right, just Slocum."

He watered Tubac. Then, trying not to limp, he walked around to the other side of the gelding and sank down on his heels across from Lydia, in the horse's purplish shadow. "You ready to talk about it yet?" he asked.

She arched a brow. "Talk about what?"

"What really happened to you back there. You've got bruises on your neck and jaw. Bruises that you couldn't have got fallin' off a horse four days ago. They're too yellow."

She snorted, and looked a bit annoyed. "Well, aren't you the observant one?"

He shrugged. "If you're not ready to talk about it, it's all right by me. I was just being sociable, that's all. And it might help you to talk about it. Been my experience that ladies like to say out whatever's botherin' 'em. Makes 'em feel better to get if off their chests."

She just looked at him.

He shrugged again. "Fine," he said finally. "How long before you gotta feed that little tyke again?"

This time, it was her turn to shrug. "I haven't the slightest idea. I supposed he'll let me know."

And then, right on cue, the baby started to fuss a little, then a little more. Slocum retrieved his bottle again, and this time Lydia thinned the milk down with even more water.

"Sorry, little Ty," he heard her mutter as she gave the infant his bottle. "We've got to make this silly stuff stretch till we get to Cross Point. Maybe they'll have a cow there. Or a goat! Wouldn't you like some nice goat milk, baby?"

It didn't seem to matter. Hungrily, Ty suckled at his watered milk.

Slocum took a drink from the canteen, then offered it to Lydia. She shook her head no. "Later," she said, her attention on the baby.

"Fine," Slocum grumbled. "Don't talk. Don't drink. Don't suppose you want anything to eat, either."

She looked up. "Eat? What do you have?"

"Not much. But I've got some jerky to spare if you want somethin' to gnaw on. Don't usually stop for a midday meal."

"What do you do for supper when you're . . . out here?" she asked

"Figured on stew," he replied, standing up. Christ, his legs were sore! Tubac was just going to have to carry double for a while, that was all there was to it. "When it gets around time to camp, I'll shoot a jackrabbit or a couple of quail."

"I have a few vegetables," she offered. "And some seasonings. Not much, but enough to fix a pot of stew. I had to leave so much behind when my horse died. I couldn't carry it all."

"And water was more important," Slocum said for her. He went to Tubac and rifled around in the saddlebag until he found a couple good-sized chunks of jerky. He brushed the lint off of one of them, and picked off a glob of dried fat.

"Yes, it was," she said. "Especially when I lost my bearings in the dust storm and fell and spilled half of it. I knew it was dry country, but back home we had a well. There was always enough."

Slocum handed her the cleaned piece of jerky. "Don't matter. I've got plenty."

She took the dried meat with a nod of thanks, but she didn't eat it. She just held it while she steadied the nursing Tyler.

Staring at his little face and not at Slocum, she said quietly, "My husband's name was Winston West. At least, that's what he told me. We had a ranch outside of a town that isn't there anymore. I should have known. I should have known when he didn't move on with the rest of them. I should have known when he didn't seem to know a shoat from a boar hog or a bull from a steer."

Slocum furrowed his brow, but held his silence. He just waited.

"Turned out he wasn't Winston West at all," she went on, still looking at the baby. "He also wasn't a rancher."

She looked up, at last, and directly into Slocum's eyes. "Would you like to know what he was? Who he was?"

Slocum said quietly, "If you're of a mind to tell me."

"His name was the Show Low Kid, and he was a bank robber and a murderer."

Stunned into silence, Slocum said nothing. He knew about Billy Cree, all right.

"I found it out the day he died," she said. She spoke matter-of-factly, without any display of emotion. "Some of his old gang tracked him down, trailed him right down to our ranch. And they killed him thirty feet from our front door. Just shot him dead, without a word. Billy Cree was the one in charge. There were two others with him."

"I'm sorry, Lydia," Slocum managed to say. "Right sorry. How'd you find out? Cree?"

She nodded.

"I heard of the Show Low Kid. Heard tell that his true name was Bob Winston. So he told you a part truth, anyway."

"Bob Winston. It's a small comfort," she said as she hoisted baby Tyler up on her shoulder and began to pat his back, jerky still in her hand, and rock him gently. Then, in the same tone, she resumed.

"They raped me," she said, just like another woman might say *it rained today*. "All three of them, over and over. It was pretty bad, but not so bad as you might think. Before Winston married me, I . . ." She paused, biting at her lower lip for an instant.

"Well," she continued at last, "I was in a line of work where I was used to being used and shoved around. Can't say I liked being reminded of it, though."

She paused again and pursed her lips. "No, I didn't like being reminded of it at all. And they'd killed my husband. Even though he'd lied to me from the day we met about dang near everything, and even if I never really loved him, I . . . I still owed him something, didn't I?"

Slocum didn't answer. She must not have expected him to, because she continued, "So the next morning, when they'd finished with me and were out in the parlor, deciding whether they'd allow me to live or die, I crawled up out of that bed and found a couple of guns. Those boys were sure surprised, all right. Even after they were dead, they still looked surprised."

She smiled at that, and Slocum felt himself shiver involuntarily.

Simultaneously, the baby let out a very loud burp, and she lowered him to her lap, saying, "There's a good baby. Slocum, can you bring me his case?" she asked. "He's wet. Or something."

If it was "something," Slocum was awfully glad that she was the one who was going to deal with it, and not him. He pulled the baby's kit down from behind his saddle and handed it over.

"No," she said, waving it off. "Just get me out a diaper." She was already unpinning the cloth she'd just put on him a couple of hours ago.

"Sure. Lydia, I'm awful sorry you got treated so raw. I mean that."

"I believe you do," she said quite seriously. "Thank you, Slocum. My diaper?"

Slocum dug through the kit and pulled free one of the folded white diapers. And when he did, something came with it.

He handed Lydia the cloth, and reached down for the papers that had fluttered to the desert floor, separating as they fell.

"So anyhow," she continued as she cleaned the baby's backside on the old diaper, tossed it aside, and settled the new one beneath him, "I covered up Winston the best I could and shooed out the livestock, and you know the rest. That's the long and short of it."

Slocum hardly heard her. He was staring at the papers in his hands.

"Slocum?" she said. "What is it?"

Slowly, he folded the papers, then shoved his hat back with a thumb. "Lydia, I think we ought to be treatin' little Tyler, there, with more respect."

Lydia cocked her head.

"The way I figure it," Slocum said, "he's about the richest baby in the Territory."

5

Ed Frame, brother to Charlie, hadn't had much luck so far.

He'd seen a lone chestnut horse dragging the remnants of a harness and suspected it was the last of that poor Mr. Tyler's team. He didn't chase it down. He didn't have to. The horse just stood there while he eased up to it.

Well, nobody could say he wasn't a kindly man. He'd stripped the rest of the tack off it, and only then did he realize the reason the horse seemed so docile: Its hind legs were tangled in a loop of leather, and it couldn't move.

So, using his pocketknife, he'd cut it free, and on top of that he'd given it some water. Not too much, though. He didn't have a lot to spare.

The horse had followed him doggedly for about a half a mile after that. He'd had to make a run at it and whoop and holler before it took off the other way.

Anyhow, he was beginning to think that this plan of Charlie's was no damn good. He hadn't wanted to kill Mr. Tyler in the first place. Why, he'd been all for going back to the wagon with Tyler and seeing what he and Charlie could do to help.

But that Charlie . . .

Sadly, Ed shook his head. Charlie was always up for a little plan for making money, and the one involving the least amount of work always called to him the strongest. It was a character flaw, Ed guessed, although he'd never said as much out loud. After all, when your older brother told you to do something, you did it—if you knew what was good for you, leastwise.

Once Mr. Justin Tyler, late of Texas and bound for California, had stupidly poured his heart out to them—all about his troubles and his wife and his coming baby and his dead uncle leaving him a gold mine out in California—Charlie had been nice and poured coffee down him and fed him the last of their ham and fixings, then shot him in his sleep.

Charlie liked everything to be easy.

Not that Ed would have stopped him, let alone tried to. He'd learned long ago that you didn't mess with Charlie when he had dollar signs in his eyes, or when he was in one of his moods. And that night, both those things were going on.

Right about now, though, Ed was thinking that maybe he'd just turn his horse around and head up north, toward Nevada. It would be nice to just leave old Charlie behind.

It would be a relief, actually. Sometimes he didn't agree with what Charlie did, or what Charlie told him to do. Of course, he'd never said a word to Charlie. Mainly because he liked living.

He reined in his horse and sat there a few seconds, considering.

Then he shook his head again. "Nah," he said to no one. "You can't run out on Charlie. You can't run out on your one and only brother. Besides, he'd probably run you down and slit your throat, anyhow."

He clucked to the horse. He guessed he'd just head straight for Cross Point, and he also guessed he wouldn't look too hard for that wagon. Hell, he'd probably already missed it, anyhow.

He sort of hoped that Charlie had, too.

He reined his horse to make a beeline for Cross Point and started off at a slow jog. No use in wearing his horse out, even though he had plenty of water. Hell, he'd probably beat Charlie—who was probably turning over every bush and cactus—to town by a couple of days, anyhow.

He had gone about a half-mile and was just breasting a low rise in the desert floor when he pulled up short. He reached for his spyglass, opened it, and held it to his eye.

"I'll be double-damned," he muttered, and took another hard look, just to make sure.

It was a leopard Appaloosa horse, carrying two people: a big man and a fair-haired woman.

No, cancel that. There were three people, because the woman was carrying a baby in her arms.

Now, this was just too much of a coincidence to let it slip by. How many babies could there be out here, smack dab in the hard, dead center of nowhere?

Their horse wasn't moving very fast, just sort of ambling along at a walk. Ed supposed that those folks weren't in much of a hurry, either. Probably taking it easy for the woman's sake, if she'd just had herself a baby.

It beat him how some drifter had run across Mrs. Tyler and her baby, but it was a funny world. Too funny, sometimes.

Oh well. Charlie'd be right proud of him.

He sighed.

While he collapsed the spyglass and put it away, he tried to figure out just how to handle this new situation. He supposed he could just ride right up to them, all friendly-like, then try to delay them until Charlie caught up with them.

Charlie was always the better one at killing folks, after all.

And Ed? He didn't have much stomach for killing women, especially mothers, and that fellow riding behind them on the Appy didn't exactly look like he'd be any picnic to put away.

Maybe he'd be better off just to trail them from a decent distance. But then, what if Charlie didn't catch up until after they'd hit town?

That wouldn't be good. Not good at all, he thought with a shake of his head.

No, he decided. He'd best ride down there and act all friendly. Just good, old, salt-of-the-earth Ed Frame, that was him. Glad to do anybody in trouble a favor, yes, ma'am and yes, sir.

Putting on his best howdy-glad-to-meet-you face, Ed Frame started down the gentle slope and toward the travelers at a soft lope.

Lydia, despite all that had recently happened to her, found herself drawn to Slocum. This surprised her to no end. She would have suspected—no, sworn—that it would be a very long time indeed before she ever found herself attracted to a man again. Billy Cree and his friends had been animals, certainly. And before that, for two long years, Winston had only been a passable lover.

Now that she thought about it, Winston sometimes exhibited a little of that feral streak that Cree and his buddies hadn't bothered to try to cover up.

No one could accuse her of being cold toward men in general after all that.

But somehow, without making one single overt move, Slocum was worming his way into her lonely heart.

He'd been nothing but a gentleman since he first picked her up. She supposed he'd saved her life, really. She didn't think the way she was feeling had anything to do with that, though.

Just listening to the tone of his voice when he talked

to her or the baby, witnessing his self-assured manner, and watching his big hands on the reins had her as wet and slippery as algaed weeds in a forest pond. He made her feel like she hadn't felt in too many years to remember, back before she'd married Winston, before she'd fallen into the trade. Why, he made her feel like a teen-aged girl again!

Now wasn't that strange?

Then again, not really, she supposed after further thought. Slocum didn't strike her as the type of man she could settle down with. He wasn't the sort that any woman could settle down with.

He just didn't appear to be the settling kind, period. And of course, that had always been the type she was most attracted to.

Which explained why she was currently about to slip and slide right out of the saddle.

"We've got company," he said, and the rumble of it startled her. She'd been looking at his powerful hands, feeling his strong arm wrapped around her, feeling his heartbeat through layers of clothing when she leaned back into him.

She twisted her head to face the direction in which he was looking, and saw a rider loping toward them. One of his hands was up in the air, waving.

Slocum stopped the horse and turned it around to face him. "Grab that baby tight," he whispered in her ear.

She knew that he meant he might have to wheel the horse in a hurry, and she held little Ty more firmly in one arm, and grasped the saddle horn with the other.

The rider didn't appear menacing, though. As he neared, she saw that he had a big grin on his face. He seemed awfully relieved to see them, in fact.

But behind her, Slocum had tensed. She glanced down to her right, and saw that his free hand was hovering near his gun, and that he'd already thumbed off the little strap that held it in its holster.

The rider whoaed his horse about ten feet out and said, with a big grin, "Howdy, folks! I sure didn't figure to run across company clear out here!"

"Good afternoon, sir," Lydia said, and behind her, Slocum grunted. She wished she could see his face.

"Where you all headed?" the man went on. He was youngish—maybe twenty-five or so—tall and fair, reasonably good-looking, and had a large and bushy yellow mustache.

"I'm goin' to Cross Point, myself," he went on, pointing to the east. "How long you folks been out here? You get caught up in that hellacious dust storm, same as me? Law, I thought me and my horse, here, would choke to death before it was over. Couldn't see more'n a few feet!"

Then, before she or Slocum could answer any of his questions, he gave his head a twist and said, "Say! You folks got you a baby in there?"

Slocum didn't answer that. Instead, he said, "We've been out a few days. I'm Slocum. This lady is Mrs. West."

The blond man tipped his hat. "Pleased," he said. "I'm Ed. Ed Frame. Happy to meet the both of you."

"We're going to Cross Point, too, Mr. Frame," Lydia said, mostly to fill the empty air that Slocum's silence left.

"Say, that's great!" replied Mr. Frame, and then he added, "And just call me Ed, ma'am. You, too, Mr. West."

"I ain't Mr. West," Slocum growled.

"No offense," Ed said quickly. "I just figured, what with the baby and all . . . What'd she say your name was?"

"Slocum," came his terse reply.

"That's all of it?"

Behind her, Slocum grunted again.

Lydia couldn't decide why Slocum seemed so skeptical

of their new traveling companion and why he had only offered her surname in his introduction. Ed seemed a like-able enough fellow to her.

Unless . . .

She felt another soft gush of warmth between her legs. Why, Slocum was as attracted to her as she was to him! Of course he wouldn't want a third wheel hanging around!

At least, that's what she hoped it was.

But there wasn't a blessed thing she could do about it. It was between the two men. So she just sat there in the saddle, holding the sleeping baby. No, that was the sleep-ing *rich* baby, she reminded herself. The deed to a gold mine, hidden in his diapers! Now, that was something, wasn't it?

"You folks mind if I travel along with y'all?" Ed asked. He patted the water bag hanging from his saddle horn. "I won't be a burden. Got my own water and my own grub. I'd sure admire the company."

"Suit yourself," Slocum said grudgingly. "We'll be travelin' slow."

"Oh, sure," Ed replied, rapidly nodding his head. "I understand. On account of the little one and all."

Right about then, Charlie Frame was running across the place where Slocum had picked up Lydia.

Charlie, who was a pretty fair tracker, knew it was a woman because her shoe size was so tiny. Also, she didn't make much of a dent in the dirt, so she couldn't have weighed more than a hundred and ten pounds or so.

She'd been on foot when the man found her, and the two of them had stayed here for a while. They'd tossed away a used diaper, too, so he knew that the man still had the kid with him. It fluttered, clean side-out, caught on a thistle bush.

Then the woman—and probably the baby, too—had mounted up on the horse, and the man had set off toward Cross Point once again, leading his nag.

Charlie shook his head. "This goddamn sonofabitch is just too good to be true," he muttered. "First he saves that baby, and now he's rescuing stranded women and lettin' 'em ride his horse. Christ on an ever-loving crutch!"

With a creak of saddle leather, Charlie stepped back up on his horse. "This do-goodin' hombre is gonna be the death of me, yet," he said as he nudged his horse in the ribs.

They started out on the trail once more.

6

Ed was about to give up on Slocum ever talking to him.

The woman? That was different. She was pleasant enough. Not exactly a chatterbox, but at least she was polite without making a fellow feel like some kind of interloper.

Which was, of course, exactly what he was.

He was getting worried, because they kept getting closer and closer to town, and there was still no sign of Charlie. Of course, he figured they'd have to camp. Even then, they might not get to Cross Point until the next night. Ed wasn't exactly sure where Cross Point was, but if Slocum kept up this pace, they might have to camp two nights.

So Ed decided to put off killing Slocum until tomorrow morning. He did this with a great sense of relief. As he'd thought when he'd first sighted them, killing Slocum wasn't going to be any picnic.

He'd decided to wait until just before dawn, when the big man was still sleeping.

That was the safest. And then he'd almost get himself a full night's sleep. Ed could be right groggy if he didn't get enough sleep. He was afraid that if he tried to wake himself up in the middle of the night to do a serious job of work, he'd be just as apt to shoot a rock or a bush as Slocum.

Also, waiting until morning would save a lot of crying and carrying on from the woman, too. Even Ed could tell that she was a little stuck on Slocum. It was just something about the way she sat there, riding in front of him. Something about the way she leaned back into him, but not too much. Something about the way she watched his hand on the reins.

He'd got just a peek at the baby, too. He had no idea people could be so ugly when they were fresh-born. The kid was all scrunched up in the face, and his head was kind of misshapen.

Mrs. West had explained to him that it was just from his "jaunt through the birth canal," whatever that meant, and that his head would look normal in a few days. Ed didn't believe her, though.

How could being born warp a baby's skull, for crying out loud?

Ed figured secretly that Mrs. West didn't know a whole lot more about babies than he did, that being somewhere between zero and nada.

He chanced another peek over his shoulder, just in case Charlie had appeared on the horizon in the last five minutes. He hadn't, though.

He said, "When you folks figure on stoppin' to set up camp?"

It was late afternoon, after all. The shadows they cast as they moved toward the eastern hills were long and narrow.

"Right about now," Slocum said, surprising him. "Let's head over toward that pile of boulders." He pointed.

"Fine with me," said Ed, and smiled.

It figured that Slocum would pick the place with the most protection from the elements. And the most protection from Charlie. Even though he didn't exactly know that Charlie was out there somewhere, hunting for that baby Mrs. West was hanging on to so tightly.

"It'll feel good to stop," Mrs. West said. She looked pretty tired.

She'd told him how she came to be out here—her man had died, she'd said, and she got lost in the storm while walking to town—and so he figured she had a right to be worn out.

"Yes, ma'am, it sure will," he replied.

Slocum said nothing.

They were fairly close to those hills. Ed was glad they were camping here, before they got up into them, because he didn't know that Charlie would be able to track them. Not that Charlie wasn't a good tracker. He was very good. But Ed had been through those hills before a long time ago, and knew they were made up of hard ground and shale and granite, and didn't hold a track worth squat.

If he had things his way, he'd have everything taken care of by the time Charlie caught up.

Well, everything except Mrs. West. No matter what ol' Charlie said, Ed wasn't going to kill her. No way in hell would he do that. Charlie could just handle that part himself.

Slocum whoaed up his horse and stepped down. Ed stopped, too. He'd been too busy thinking and gazing ahead into the distance to realize that they were already to the boulders. They were bigger when you got up on them than they'd looked from a distance.

While Slocum took the baby from Mrs. West and helped her down, Ed took a last look back at the horizon—no Charlie, yet—and dismounted.

He smiled. "You want I should take care of the horses, Slocum?" he asked.

•   •   •   •

Slocum didn't trust this Ed Frame any farther than he could pick him up and throw him, which he reckoned was about ten feet. Too goddamn smiley, for one thing.

Slocum had put him on firewood duty and seen to the horses himself. Ed Frame rode a tall, slab-sided, bay gelding, whose condition told Slocum that Ed had been out in the storm, all right, so that part of his story was true. Slocum must have curried a good pound of dust and grit out of his coat. Curried out a good deal of long-dead coat, too.

Ed Frame also didn't believe in graining his horse much, if at all. He didn't carry any grain on him, and when Slocum fed the gelding a measure of Tubac's oats, he practically inhaled them.

By the time Slocum walked over to the pile of firewood that Ed was just coaxing into flame, Slocum was as mad as a wet hen. It didn't help when Ed looked up with that big, stupid grin on his face, and said, "Howdy, pardner!"

"I ain't your partner, Frame," Slocum growled, and resisted the urge to punch him out. The resistance was more for Lydia's sake than Ed Frame's. But any man who didn't take decent care of his own horse was a jackass in Slocum's book. Probably worse.

Why, that horse hadn't had a good groom—or a good feed—in a coon's age!

Frame's face went slack for just a second. But the grin popped back as if it had never faded.

"Why, sorry there, Slocum," he said apologetically. "I guess I ain't known you long enough to call you my pard."

"How's the kid?" Slocum asked Lydia, pointedly ignoring Frame's half-assed apology.

Lydia, who had refilled the baby's little bottle with more of the thinned canned milk, was feeding him. She looked up from his greedy little face.

"He's just fine, Slocum," she said, keeping her voice

soothing. "Well, as fine as can be expected. He'll be a lot better once we get to Cross Point, though. How much longer will it be, do you suppose?"

"Depends on those hills," he said, nodding toward the east. The hills, looming only a moment before, were now little more than fading shadows against a darkening sky. All the color and fire of the Arizona sunset was to the west.

"As I remember, they're kind of tricky," he added.

"Tricky, how?" she asked.

"There's no one pass," he replied. "Just several trails that are hard to follow, because the terrain's so rough and rocky. Lots of caves. Most of 'em are full of bats and some of 'em come with cougars. Lots of dead ends."

Surprisingly, Lydia smiled. "You make it sound so enticing, Slocum."

He didn't quite know what to say.

But Ed Frame did. "Oh, them hills ain't so hard to navigate."

Slocum turned toward him, one brow cocked. "You been through here recently, Frame?"

Ed Frame shook his head quickly. "Oh, no. Not recent-like. But I been through them hills lots of times. I can lead the way, if'n you want."

"We'll see," Slocum said flatly. He had a bad feeling about Frame to start with, and it was gnawing at him more all the time. He particularly didn't want to put his fate into Frame's hands. He just wanted to stall the sonofabitch until he could think of something better.

Other than a bullet to the head, that was. That might get him on Lydia's bad side, and he was too drawn to her to want that in any way, shape, or form.

In fact, it had been about all he could do to keep from cupping one of those high, round breasts of hers in his hand while they were riding along. He'd had a hard-on for about half the time, too. She'd kept on leaning back into him, and she was so pretty and wheat-blond and she was so soft . . .

"What's for supper?" Ed asked.

"Thought you said you had your own grub," Slocum snapped.

Lydia said, "Can't we share, Slocum?"

By the tone of her voice, Slocum knew that she was aware there was tension between him and Ed. At least she hadn't mentioned that deed they'd found with the baby's things. Slocum was certain he didn't trust Ed Frame with that information.

He pushed his anger back down. "I didn't shoot any game," he replied, "on account of little Tyler, there. We'll have to make do with what's in the possibles bag."

"That's fine with me," Lydia said. "I've got a little food left in my bag, too. Three boiled eggs, a little coffee—"

"*Real* coffee?" Ed interrupted.

"Certainly," said Lydia, as if she'd never settle for less. "Arbuckle's."

Ed took off his hat and slapped it across his chest. "Hell, ma'am, I ain't drunk nothin' but burnt and boiled grain for weeks. I swan, real live Arbuckle's! You're a regular goddess, Mrs. West."

And Lydia, dad-blast her, blushed.

Another reason to dislike Ed Frame.

It was getting to be a pretty long list.

It was too dark to track them any farther, but Charlie Frame wasn't worried, not by a long shot. Their trail had met up with a lone rider's several hundred yards back, and by the way the rider's horse toed in just a tad in front, Charlie knew who it belonged to.

His little brother, Ed.

Charlie leaned back against his bedroll, took another chaw off his jerky, and smiled. Unlike his brother's open, stupid grin, it was a calculating expression. But then, Charlie was a calculating man.

He figured that Ed had just sort of joined up with them. A fellow pilgrim, so to speak.

He leaned forward, toward his little fire, and poured himself a cup of coffee. Or what passed for it. He didn't figure he could afford to take a chance on a very big fire, but he hankered for something hot to drink, even if it tasted like shit.

As it had turned out, he didn't need to worry about his little fire alerting anybody. It had gone all the way dark by this time, and he couldn't see even a hint of their fire.

Oh well. He'd catch up with them tomorrow. Then he'd take care of what Ed had no stomach for. He wondered if they'd make the hills before he caught up. He supposed so. It couldn't be helped.

But he knew the same trails through those hills that Ed did, knew 'em by heart. He took a long drink of bitter coffee, then leaned back again.

Hell, he wished he'd shot himself something for supper. Couldn't take a chance on firing a shot out here, though. Sound carried a pretty far piece.

Musty-tasting jerky, crumbly hardtack, and bad coffee, that's what he'd settle for tonight. But tomorrow? That would be different, all right.

Lydia could sure slap together a good dinner out of next to nothing, Slocum thought as he mopped his plate with a biscuit.

It turned out that she'd had some scraps of ham left on her, and between her ham and her fixings and his fixings—and the donation of a little salt and pepper from Ed Frame—she'd stirred them up a pot of thick ham-and-bean soup and made up a pan of feather-light biscuits to go alongside it. She even had a little pot of raspberry jelly to go with them.

They'd gone through two pots of coffee, too. He figured that Ed Frame had downed at least one and a half of them by his lonesome. He'd also eaten nearly half of their soup.

Lydia had slid Slocum a glance and a surprisingly fetching roll of her eyes when ol' Ed dived in for thirds.

That single glance of hers made it almost worth eating with a pig.

'Course, he couldn't do anything about it. Not with Ed Frame hanging around. But Slocum was sure stirred up, all right. He was, in fact, about to get himself a bad case of the blue balls.

Lydia leaned over and took his plate. She smiled. "I believe I won't even have to clean this one, Slocum. It appears you've already done it for me."

Before Slocum could reply, an eager Ed Frame piped up, "I done better than that, Mrs. West. I licked mine clean, I did!"

Lydia turned toward him and took his outstretched plate. "That's nice, Mr. Frame, but I believe I'll wash it, anyway."

Slocum snorted.

Frame just shrugged. "Suit yourself," he said with that stupid grin.

The baby was crying.

Beneath a lonely sky filled with distant, glimmering stars, Slocum rolled over underneath his blanket and forced his eyes open. Lydia was already sitting up, he saw. The baby was in her arms, and she was rocking it, trying to soothe it.

"Diaper?" Slocum offered groggily.

"No," Lydia whispered with a shake of her head. "I guess he's hungry."

"In the goddamn middle of the night?" Slocum asked. He was tired and wanted to go back to sleep, or else he wanted Ed Frame gone so that he and Lydia could get to know each other better.

In a biblical sense, of course.

But just then Ed Frame woke up, too, and asked, "What the heck's that racket?"

"The kid's hungry," Slocum snapped.

Lydia got up and started to root around for the can of milk.

"Well, gosh, I didn't know," Ed Frame said apologetically. "It's the gol-dang middle of the night! Can't he wait till breakfast, like the rest of us?"

"Babies have tiny stomachs," Lydia said. She poured a couple inches of milk into the bottle, then topped it off with water from a canteen. "And they're brand-new. They're not supposed to know about things like breakfast and dinner times. I think."

She offered the bottle, and little Ty took it greedily. Just the sound of that baby sucking at that bottle reminded Slocum that he'd like to be at Lydia's breast, for real, and his pants felt suddenly tighter. He shifted uncomfortably.

Across the fire, Ed Frame yanked his blanket over his head and rolled away, muttering, "Finally!"

Slocum stared at him for a moment, mostly to take his mind off of Lydia's charms, then said to her, "For somebody who don't know nothin' about babies, I'd say you're doin' right by him."

She shrugged her pretty shoulders. "Just common sense, that's all. He's got the prettiest hair! Was his mama a redhead, too?"

"No," said Slocum. "She was dark. Brown hair and brown eyes. There was a picture of both his folks, though. His daddy had light hair. Might have been red. Want to see it?"

"Surely," Lydia replied, her smile soft. "I'd like to very much."

Slocum reached over his head toward his saddlebags

and dragged them around. After a little digging by the light of the campfire, he pulled out the photograph and handed it over.

When he did, his fingers touched Lydia's. He could have sworn they sparked.

Lydia must have felt the same thing, too, because a look of surprise crossed her face, just for a split second.

She didn't remark on it, though. She merely pulled the photograph toward her, then tilted it so that the fire lit its surface.

"Yes," she whispered after a moment. "Yes, it could have been red. Strawberry blond, perhaps." She handed it back, this time careful to avoid bodily contact with Slocum. "I believe he looks like his daddy," she added.

Slocum squinted at the picture. "How the hell can you tell?"

She laughed with a soft chuckle that burrowed inside him. "All babies look alike, right?"

He nodded.

"I thought so, too, until I got to studying Tyler, here," she said. The baby was still working eagerly at the bottle, and this time her gentle smile was for him. "He's beautiful. I don't believe there's ever been another baby quite like him."

Slocum gave a good-natured snort.

"Oh hush," she admonished him, but she was smiling as she said it. "Don't go thinking I've gone all soft." She looked down at the child in her arms once more. "Well, maybe just a little bit. Right, Tyler?"

Slocum half expected her to make cootchie-cootchie noises at the baby, and the sad thing was that in his present condition, he would have found that sexually enticing, too.

He had it bad, all right.

Lydia set the empty bottle aside and lifted the baby to her shoulder. Softly patting his back, she leaned forward a bit and slid a glance over toward the sleeping Ed Frame.

"You don't trust him, do you?" she whispered.

"Not rightly," Slocum replied. She was smarter than he'd credited her with. In a lower tone, he whispered, "Don't even trust him to be asleep."

She nodded her understanding and sat back. Just then, the baby burped, a tiny sound, and she brought him back down into her arms again. Gently, she began to rock him back and forth.

"Won't be long before you're fast asleep, Ty," she murmured. And then she looked up at Slocum.

"We won't make Cross Point before nightfall tomorrow, will we?" she asked. "I've traveled this route with Winston a couple times, and it seems to me like we're making slow headway."

Slocum nodded. "I think you're right. If we had another horse, it might be different. But I don't want to push Tubac too hard. We got enough milk?"

She shrugged. "There's maybe a little less than half a can left. It would have helped if you'd known to thin it down when you first fed him."

"Sorry," said Slocum.

"I think it'll be all right," she replied, and gave him another pretty smile. "He's a fat baby. Must be almost nine pounds. He might get a little grouchy, but he'll make it fine, so long as we don't run in to any unnecessary delays."

She began to hum to the baby, which Slocum took as his cue to roll back over and try to go to sleep. The emphasis being on "try."

Ed Frame, beneath the cover of his blanket, smiled to himself. He figured that Charlie wasn't close behind. And Charlie was going to prove to be an "unnecessary delay," all right.

Ed had decided for sure not to try to shoot Slocum in

his sleep, or in the morning. For one thing, Ed didn't like to get up early, not for anybody.

He'd decided to do it on the trail, tomorrow.

Now, Ed knew that Slocum didn't trust him, which was why he'd offered to trailblaze once they got into the hills. He figured that, having offered, there wasn't any way Slocum would let him lead the way.

And behind was where he wanted to be.

After all, you couldn't very well shoot a man in the back while you were in front of him, now could you?

7

Miles to the southwest on the old Winston West spread, Billy Cree, a drying, blood-soaked dish towel wrapped around his head, finally decided that he was strong enough to ride.

And to get that bitch.

His horse, which had come back all by itself, was in the corral, along with Randy's. He didn't know where the hell Wes's had got to. His boys, Randy and Wes, lay beneath hastily and painfully carried rocks out in the yard, near what he supposed was the Kid's mound. Damn him anyway.

Those slugs Lydia fired had split the side of his head, bringing on a long state of unconsciousness from which he supposed he was lucky to have awakened. ·

By then it was too late, though. Wes and Randy were dead and beginning to stink up the place, and Mrs. Show Low Kid was long gone. And then, of course, there was the wind.

He'd waited it out. And while he was waiting, he'd stitched up his own head with hairs plucked from his horse's tail, and survived off a couple of chickens that had been stupid enough to hang around the place.

His head still hurt him, still pounded when he did anything strenuous—like carry those damned cairn stones, for
example—but he was alive. And that was the main thing,
wasn't it?

His vision was a little cockeyed for a day or two. He
couldn't hit the side of the barn, for starters. But by now
it was almost as good as before.

He'd done quite a bit of cogitating on the matter of
where Lydia might go off to, and had finally decided that
she'd probably gone east, over to Cross Point. And he
figured that hellacious dust storm had to have slowed her
down a good bit.

Maybe even killed her. Which would save him the
trouble.

Damned women. Nothing but trouble.

He loaded up his horse, said a word or two over Wes's
and Randy's makeshift graves, slung a vitriolic curse toward the Kid's, and set off at a jog.

Slocum, Lydia, baby Tyler, and Ed Frame were just about
to start climbing up into the hills. And much to Ed's surprise, Slocum had put him in the lead, which fouled up
Ed's plans any way you looked at it.

"You still back there?" he called when he rounded a
bend and found himself alone.

In half a second, that Appy's nose came into sight, and
the rest of him followed, bearing Slocum and Lydia. And
the baby, naturally.

"Don't worry about us," Slocum shouted. He didn't
appear any too jovial. "Just keep on going and we'll keep
following."

Goddamn him, anyway.

Last night, Ed had been sure that he would have had
plenty of opportunities to blast Slocum's head open by
now. Maybe Slocum was on to him. Ed couldn't figure

how, but Slocum seemed half-psychic about some things. Mayhap this was one of them.

But then, if Slocum had somehow figured out what he was doing, why hadn't Slocum killed him? Or tried to, at least.

It was a puzzlement.

Ed just hoped that Charlie wasn't far behind. For instance, close enough that he could pop Slocum in the back of the skull and they could just get on with it.

Ed wasn't too crazy about the killing parts of this deal, but the more he thought about it, two deaths didn't seem like too much of a price to pay for that gold mine the kid had.

Still, he'd feel a lot better if he didn't have to do it. Kill anybody, that was. Especially that nice Mrs. West. She was awful pretty.

Not that what she looked like would matter one whit to Charlie, Ed reminded himself.

The sky had gone all squirrelly about an hour and a half ago, and that bothered Ed, too. By now, it had turned the color of a dirty nickel, was dull yellow in places, and had altogether gone an awful lot darker than it should be.

He supposed they were in for another blow. He wasn't any too happy about it.

It wasn't blowing yet, though, and when he'd asked Slocum about it, and hadn't they better stop, Slocum had just grunted at him and waved him on. 'Course, that had been about twenty minutes ago.

Considering the way the big man seemed to feel about him, Ed didn't press the question again. They'd stop when Slocum wanted to stop.

It was no skin off Ed's nose, one way or the other. Slocum was going to end up just as dead, and the lady, too.

But where the hell was Charlie?

• • •

As a matter of fact, Charlie had trailed them to the point where they entered the hills, seen the path that Ed was taking, and promptly circled around.

At the moment, he was in front of them, flat on his belly on a rock above a particular narrow pass, with his spyglass to his eye.

Only one thing worried him. Not his bringing down the big man, of course. He had surprise on his side, and he was a pretty damn good shot, even if he did say so himself. What he was worried about was that he might not shoot the woman fast enough.

There were caves in these hills, deep caves. The only thing that tickled at his worry bone was that the woman would get her fanny—and the baby's—back into one of them. Get into one of them with a gun in her possession, that was.

Might be days before he and Ed talked her out. Or got off a clean shot.

He didn't want to take any chances on hurting that kid. At least, not until he and Ed had a chance to establish legal blood-ties to it.

Charlie snorted, despite himself. That was a laugh. But Tyler and his missus had been about fifteen hundred miles from home, and if he and Ed turned up in California with their poor orphaned niece or nephew, who was to say they were fibbing?

Especially if they went back to Cross Point first. Tyler and his wife had been through there. Not long enough to form any real ties, but long enough that they'd be remembered by the clerks at the mercantile and a few other stores.

Tyler himself had told Charlie and Ed that he and his wife had no living relatives. He said that the last of them, his wife's uncle Desmond, was the one who had left the gold mine to him and his missus. It was actively producing right now.

And Charlie had been dreaming about going out to California and wading, naked as a jaybird, into a great big pile of his gold. Well, the baby's gold.

But if the kid get sick or had an accident and croaked once he and Ed got out there and got themselves established, well, that was just too bad, now, wasn't it?

Actually, Charlie had given a good deal of thought to trying to pass himself off as the kid's father. But the modernities being what they were, he supposed it was entirely possible that Tyler had sent his wife's uncle a picture of himself. Maybe a wedding picture or something. And miners, not being overburdened with possessions, tended to show those things off.

No, he and Ed were better off just playing the roles of shirt-tail cousins—second or third cousins, he thought—who had stepped in and dutifully taken over responsibility for the kid after the tragic deaths of Mr. and Mrs. Tyler.

May they rest in peace.

Why, even Charlie was close to wiping away a tear as he thought about how they'd introduce themselves.

He peered though his spyglass again. Still not a damned thing.

He hadn't heard a shot, so he figured that either Ed couldn't line one up, or else—like usual—he'd chickened out on doing the dirty work. Ed was his baby brother and all, but it was getting goddamn wearing, this reticent tendency of his.

Charlie might have called any other man a coward, but Ed was his only brother. A man couldn't exactly call his own brother a coward, could he? Mainly because it would reflect pretty badly on him.

"Hurry the hell up, Ed," Charlie muttered, and went back to staring through his spyglass.

"Stop," Slocum said, and Ed pulled up his horse without thinking.

He craned around to see Slocum just sitting there, his brow furrowed.

"What?" Ed asked.

Slocum waved a hand. "Just wait." Slowly, he turned his head from side to side, as if searching for something or someone.

Ed began to wonder if this Slocum bird wasn't something besides a saddle bum. He sure had instincts, all right. What Charlie called instincts, anyway. It was all Ed could do not to join in with Slocum and eyeball the surrounding rocks.

He held off, though, and smiled to himself. Maybe Charlie was close, after all.

"What?" Ed Frame asked.

Slocum growled "Just wait," and waved him off. He had a real bad feeling about this.

It had been growing on him for some time, but ever since they'd turned down this particular pass, it had gotten considerably stronger.

Ed was leading them in the right direction. Slocum hadn't been through these hills all that often, but he had a mind for terrain. Things were looking familiar, and familiar in the right order.

So, if Ed Frame wasn't up to something, what was tickling at the hairs on the back of his neck?

Finally, Slocum said, "All right," and Ed Frame started forward again. Slocum, with Lydia and the baby before him, left a good distance between Tubac and the backside of Ed's horse.

"What's the matter?" Lydia whispered.

"Don't rightly know," Slocum replied. He was scanning the hills and the rocks, looking for something out of place, something to explain this feeling of his. "Somethin' ain't on the up and up, though."

"You'll protect us," Lydia said, as if she truly believed it.

He wished he could.

At last they came into sight, and Charlie Frame broke out in a grin.

Not for long, though. His damned little brother was in the lead, and furthermore, the big man was riding the woman double. Plus, she was carrying that baby like a shield.

Now, wasn't that just his luck?

He'd have to wait until they passed him down below to get a clean shot at that hombre, and even then he'd have to aim for the shoulder. He couldn't take a chance on the slug going right though the big man and wounding the woman, because she just might fall off the stupid horse and land smack on the baby.

He needed that baby alive.

For the time being.

8

Slocum felt a familiar sharp, searing pain in his shoulder before he heard the shot.

He nearly tumbled off Tubac, but caught himself and tightly gripped the saddle horn. With the other, he wheeled Tubac around. Ignoring both the fire in his shoulder and Lydia's surprised scream, he sent Tubac flying back down the pass.

He heard another shot—a handgun, this time—then a second rifle shot. Both missed him, but one slug sang off the rocks ahead, splintering them.

He had to make a fast decision: whether to try for the end of the canyon and the shelter of the bend—and risk staying in the open for at least another hundred yards—or duck into that cave that yawned to the left.

He saw the dust pop up from the canyon floor ahead just before he heard the sound of the shot, and made a sharp left turn into what he hoped and prayed was an unoccupied cave.

It was, thank God.

He flung himself down off Tubac, then jerked a terrified Lydia out of the saddle and to the ground before he fanned Tubac on the rump to send him farther in. Adrenaline overcame the pain, and he then threw himself forward and down to the cave's floor and looked out over the pass.

Ed Frame wasn't anywhere in sight. It crossed his mind that Frame had been shot and that now he'd have to do something stupid, like go out there and rescue him. And then he heard a shout.

"You comin' up or am I comin' down?" A new voice. The man up in the rocks.

Slocum opened his mouth to holler something nasty back at him, but he was cut off before he could utter a word.

"Nope. You come on down, Charlie!" shouted Ed Frame.

Sonofabitch!

"That rat bastard!" Lydia shouted over the echoing cries of the baby, who had started to bawl.

"Just what I was thinkin'," Slocum growled. He crawled backward, toward her, always keeping an eye to the cave's mouth. These hills were peppered with caves and crevices, and Slocum was lucky he'd picked one that was more than a couple of feet deep. It seemed to go back a ways, too.

At least, he thought it did. He hadn't bumped into Tubac yet, anyhow.

He backed up until he was even with Lydia, who was trying to hush the child. She wasn't having much luck, though.

She glanced up, and her face was filled with worry and fright. "I don't understand! How could he possibly have sent somebody ahead? How could he know we were out here in the first place? How could he—"

Slocum cut her off. "I don't know. The thing is that he did it. That's what we've got to worry about right now. You can ask all the questions you want later on."

Slocum took his gaze from the cave's mouth long

enough to glance back over his fiery shoulder toward the rear.

It looked big enough. At the back wall, Tubac was standing about ten feet from him, which he figured made the cave about twenty-two or twenty-five feet deep. It was high enough to stand up in, too. At least, Tubac wasn't banging his head on the rocky ceiling. He was close to it, though.

And there were no bats. That was good. If he was going to spend any time at all on his belly in a cave, he'd rather it were one where he wasn't flopped in bat guano.

"You're hurt!" Lydia cried, as if she'd just noticed. Maybe she had. And then she made a peeping sound, barely audible over the baby's wails. "Oh, God! *I'm* hurt!"

She stared at her shoulder, and her eyes were round as saucers.

"No, you're not," Slocum said. There was no sign of movement out front. Ed and his buddy were probably still getting themselves arranged.

He nodded toward her shoulder. "No holes." He took a look down at his own. The bullet, which had entered his back, had exited out the front. He said, "You just got some of my blood splatter."

"Wondered why it didn't hurt," Lydia said, brows knitted. Then she looked back at Slocum again. "Can I fix that up for you?"

"You'd best quiet that kid, first," Slocum said. "I can't hear a damned thing." He tipped his head toward the cave's opening.

Lydia nodded, and Slocum left her, crawling back up toward the mouth of the cave. His shoulder hurt like hell and he needed to get his rifle out of the bag on Tubac's saddle.

But first, he wanted to take a long look out front and see what Ed and his nasty little friend were up to.

• • •

Charlie, on his gelding, skittered down the last of the sharply angled cliff face and walked up next to his waiting brother. He swung down off his horse and shouted, "What the hell were you doin', you idiot?"

Ed rose up from his squat, there in his bay's shade, and hollered back, "What'd you mean, what was I doin'? I was doin' what I was supposed to be doin', that's what! And don't you ever say hello to a person?"

Charlie rolled his eyes. Ed had always been a little slow, but this was pushing it. "Hello! And I mean ridin' out front, you lunatic! Hell, I could'a just picked him off clean if he was in front!"

He didn't add that the baby would have still been in the way. He just felt like hollering at somebody right now, and Ed was handy.

And Ed was also a fool.

"I couldn't do nothin' else," Ed said defensively, and dug his toe in the dirt. "I been tryin' to get behind him all dang morning. I even tried to trick him. You know, that newfangled reverse psychology crud that you're always talkin' about!"

Charlie sighed. "Ed, how many times I got to tell you not to try out stuff you ain't got no hope of understandin'?"

"Goddamn it, Charlie, I was just tryin'—" Ed began.

"Don't, Ed," said Charlie with a disgusted shake of his head. "Just don't. Now, where'd that sonofabitch take our little money machine to?"

Lydia finally got the baby quieted, just in time for Slocum to hear the final shouted words of Charlie and Ed's conversation. Then they lapsed into a more conversational tone, and he couldn't make out a blasted thing.

He'd learned enough, though, that he was fairly certain he and Lydia weren't going to make it out of here anytime soon. This Charlie, whoever he was, appeared to be the brains of the outfit, although admittedly, that wouldn't take a helluva lot. Slocum wouldn't be able to flummox him as easily as he'd twisted Ed around his finger.

"Slocum?" Lydia whispered. "Your shoulder?"

He didn't glance back at her. "Not yet," he said.

"But—"

He held up his hand to silence her, and the quick movement brought stabbing shards of pain once again. He fought it off though, gritted his teeth, and put all his attention on listening to the approaching crunching sounds he thought that he'd heard, just over the soft whine of wind.

Footsteps. Two men, not more. And they'd left their horses somewhere.

But before they came into sight, they stopped. Slocum swore under his breath. It would have been awful nice of them if they'd just stand out there in the clear for a second or two. Let him take them both down.

They weren't going to be that cooperative, though.

There came a soft mumble, not a word of which Slocum could make out except to tell that they were conversing, and then a shouted, "Hey, boy! You in there?"

It had been a heap of years since anybody'd had enough gall to call Slocum "boy," and he believed that he was offended by it. In fact, it sort of set his teeth on edge. He made no reply.

Then Ed's voice called out. "Hey, Slocum! You alive, or what? I heared that baby cryin', so I know it's alive!"

Once again, Slocum held his tongue. Which was a very good thing, because just then, those boys out there had themselves a right explosive conversation, a good part of which he heard.

"Slocum!" shouted the unseen Charlie. "You say Slocum?"

Ed muttered something, then Charlie set into a true hissy fit.

"Goddamn it, Ed! You mean to say we got *the* Slocum trapped in a cave and you didn't bother to let me in on it?"

"Don't hit me!" Ed shouted back.

"I ain't gonna hit you! I'm gonna kill you, that's what!"

The sounds of a scuffle came to Slocum's ears, and quickly, he whispered, "Stay put!" to Lydia. Staying low, he crept from the cave and out into the open.

He moved toward the sound of the fight, hugging the rise of the cliff wall behind him, peering around boulders and rock heaps as he went. Finally, just as he rounded a jut of rock, Ed landed right at his feet.

It surprised the living hell out of both of them.

Ed groped for his gun just as Charlie's shot chipped the rock hear Slocum's face, spattering his cheek with granite shrapnel.

His gun drawn but not fired, Slocum pulled back quickly and muttered a string of curses. Ed had scrambled to safety by then, damn it, and Slocum had no choice but to try and skinny his way back to the cave.

Swearing beneath his breath, he started back.

But Ed and Charlie weren't going to make it easy on him. Every rock pile and rock fall he rounded, every boulder he peeped out from behind, they were there in the distance, waiting for him. He had emptied his pistol before he was halfway back to the cave, and had to stop to reload. His face, already peppered with rock shards and bleeding profusely, was taking a new peppering.

Whoever that Charlie was, he was sure a good shot. Damn it.

Slocum had to empty his gun again to make it to the next boulder. Although he knew the wound wasn't serious, his shoulder was paining him something fierce. His face stung to beat the band, and he was wiping blood out of his eyes every two shakes, but the thing that was bothering him the most was not knowing what the hell these two wanted!

"Whee!" shouted Ed while Slocum crouched behind the rock and reloaded once again. "This is a regular turkey shoot, ain't it Charlie?"

And then Slocum heard a rifle's report—not from across the narrow pass, but from the cave. By this time, the opening was only twenty feet to his left.

"Get out, you sons of bitches!" Lydia shouted from the cover of the cave. "Go on, or I'll blast you to kingdom come!"

Strangely enough, a big grin momentarily widened Slocum's face. What a gal!

He shouted, "Cover me!" and when Lydia began to pop off shots as quick as a serious string of firecrackers, he scurried the rest of the way as fast as he could. He threw himself the last few feet, then rolled past Lydia into the shadows of the cave.

She stopped firing, backed up, then turned toward him.

"I take it that whatever you did, it didn't work," she said dryly.

"You take it right." Slocum panted.

"You're a mess," she said.

"Remember before?" he said. "When you asked to fix me up?"

"Offer still stands."

"All right," he said, observing the lack of any action whatsoever across the way. "Because now would be a pretty fair time."

9

Charlie wrenched the hat from his head, then slapped his thigh with it. Then he whacked Ed across the chest.

"Hey, Charlie!" yelped Ed, jumping back in surprise. "Cut that out!"

"I'm gonna hurt you a whole lot worse than that if we lose the kid," Charlie growled as he settled his hat back on.

He didn't appear to be concerned that it was crooked, and Ed didn't figure it would be too smart to point it out to him right at the moment. Instead, he started back toward where they'd ground-tied the horses.

Charlie didn't shut up, though. Dogging Ed's footsteps, he railed, "And Slocum! Man, oh, man! You sure can pick 'em, little brother."

Ed felt another whack with the hat, right across his back. He flinched a little, but he didn't comment on it. Instead, he kept on walking and said, "I don't see why you're so all-fired riled up about this Slocum character. I mean, he's big and all, but you act like he's some famous gunfighter or somethin'."

"He *is* some famous gunfighter, you badger's butt!" Charlie hollered, and Ed cringed again. "Where you been for the last ten or fifteen years that you never heard of Slocum? You spend all your time with your head up a cow's ass?"

This time, halfway to the horses, Ed stopped. He turned around. "Now you're bein' plain mean, Charlie," he said. "I never once had my head up . . . where you said. And you know it."

"Might as well've had," Charlie insisted, and his face wasn't pretty. "You sure ain't been usin' it for thinkin'. Or listenin', neither. Don't you know who Slocum *is*?"

Charlie was making him feel downright stupid again, but by this time Ed was sort of used to it.

Unfortunately.

He sighed, long and hard, then said, "No, Charlie, I don't. Why don't you tell me? I know you're just dyin' to."

Apparently exasperated, Charlie rolled his eyes. "Ed, Slocum's the man who brought down Ike Teal! The feller who broke up the Scioto County range war, singlehanded! The yahoo what brought Rex and Iggy Stout in, stone-cold dead and across the backs of their own horses! The man who—"

"I got the idea, Charlie," Ed broke in.

"—rounded up Marty Greenleaf and his whole damned gang!"

Sometimes it took Charlie a little while to run down if he was on a tear. This was one of those times.

Charlie went through a couple more rumored apprehensions and range wars and out and out killings before he finally slowed up to take a long breath, and Ed took full advantage of the situation.

"Well, now, Charlie," Ed said, starting toward the horses once more, "I'm right sorry. I guess I should hang around the bars till all hours and listen to gossip like you do."

Charlie was calmed down some at the moment, and

walking alongside him. "It ain't gossip if it's somethin' you can use. And you sure could have used it when you ran into Slocum. You should'a shot him from a distance. We could'a finished off the woman any old time!"

Ed felt a new tantrum building in his brother, and began to walk a tad faster.

Just in time, too.

"But god*damn* it, Ed!" Charlie shouted, and grabbed for his hat again.

Ed covered his head just a fraction of a second before Charlie's hat smacked it.

"Slocum!" Charlie said through gritted teeth. "Got us mixed up with goddamned *Slocum*! You beat everything, you know that?"

"There," said Lydia, and tied off the bandage. She'd managed to calm the baby and see to Slocum at the same time. Quite a feat, he thought.

While she'd tidied his wound, he sat facing the cave's opening, his rifle across his lap, so she wasn't the only one who was doing two things at once.

This didn't really occur to him, though. He was used to doing several things at the same time.

"It's a miracle you didn't fall flat on your face," she said. She lifted another rag from the little pan of water. Wringing it out, she carefully began to work on his cheek and temple. "You surely lost a lot of blood."

"Ouch!" Slocum yelped when she accidentally rubbed an imbedded rock chip the wrong way.

She gently picked it out, whispering, "Oh, hush," and went on with her ministrations. "I guess it wasn't enough to kill you, though."

"You sound kind'a disappointed," he said with a smile.

"No, not at all." She sat back. "Slocum, what on earth do those men want? They can't be after me. Or the baby."

She didn't say it, but he knew what she meant.

"I don't know," he said. "I never seen either one'a them before." Then he paused and studied her face. Damn, but she was pretty. And she also looked like she didn't quite believe him.

"Honest," he added.

Her fine brows knitted and worked before she said, "All right. It's not that I think you're lying, Slocum. It's just so crazy. This whole thing."

He said, "I've seen crazier."

One corner of her mouth quirked up into a smile. "I'll bet you have."

Slocum couldn't stand it any longer. He pulled her to him and kissed her, right then and there.

She resisted him a tad at first, but only briefly. And then she melted into his arms, into the kiss, and opened her mouth for him.

And then, halfway through that moment of madness, he remembered where they were.

He broke off the kiss.

"Slocum . . ." She breathed.

"Sorry," he said. "I didn't have any right to do that." After all, she'd been through hell these last few days. Most women wouldn't want to be touched by a man again, ever.

But amazingly, she whispered, "I liked it. I like you. You make me feel safe."

He smiled. "That's kind of lopsided thinkin'. I mean, seein' as how I've brought you nothin' but trouble since we met."

She cocked her head. "True. But then, if you hadn't come along, I might very well be dead in the desert. Everything considered, I think I'm working toward the positive side of things."

He started to speak, but just then a shout came from outside the cave, from the opposite side of the canyon.

"Hey! Slocum!" It wasn't Ed, he didn't think. It must

be the one Ed had called Charlie. To Slocum, who had caught a few glimpses of Charlie while Charlie was shooting at him a couple minutes ago, the two men appeared to be brothers.

They looked enough alike, anyhow.

"I hear you," Slocum shouted back. "What the hell do you want?" He noticed that Lydia had inched forward, and was listening.

"We want that baby," came the surprising reply. "Give it over, and we'll let you go on your way."

Lydia's brow's knotted. "What? Why on earth!" she whispered.

"What do you want with this kid?" Slocum shouted. Frankly, he was just as puzzled as she. Little Tyler had a deed to a mine, but for all Slocum knew, that mine was deader than a doornail, likely producing nothing but worthless rock.

And Ed and Charlie had no way of knowing about it, anyhow.

"Never you mind," Charlie hollered. "Just give it over."

Behind Slocum, Lydia picked up the baby again and held him close. Even if Slocum had been inclined to give in to Charlie and Ed's demands, he'd hate to think about wrestling the kid away from Lydia. Right at the moment, she looked like a mama grizzly protecting her cub.

"That'll be the day," Slocum shouted back.

"You're damn right, it will," Lydia whispered through clenched teeth.

"Have it your own way, then," Charlie called. "We can wait you out. We got more water than you. And Ed tells me you're runnin' short on milk for the kid. You want him to live, Slocum? You'll think long and hard on my offer."

"Don't need no thinkin'," Slocum shouted. "Why don't you come and get him?"

"I ain't that stupid," Charlie called. "Maybe Ed is, but I ain't. No way I'm gonna charge me a cave with the one and only Slocum holed up in it."

Something seemed to dawn on Lydia. "He knows who you are. How?"

There was an accusation in there somewhere, but Slocum didn't have time to sort it out.

"Oh, come on, Charlie," he taunted. "Give it a try!"

"Dry up," the unseen Charlie called. "I mean that literal, Slocum."

Slocum heard the sound of braying laughter, probably from Ed. Or, that Charlie. Slocum couldn't wait to get his hands on him. As it was, he couldn't make out hide nor hair of him. Ed, either. He would have given most anything for a clean shot right about now.

"Ed your brother, Charlie?" Slocum hollered.

"Reckon I'm bound to claim him," came the reply.

"Reckon you'd best," Slocum called. "Nobody else would."

A shot rang out, and rock chips sprayed from the ceiling of the cave.

Lydia immediately dived to the side, sheltering the baby's body with hers, and hissing, "Don't go pissing them off, Slocum."

"Just needling a little bit," he said, smirking.

"Just don't needle us to death."

Billy Cree, who had switched horses twice, found the spot where Lydia's horse lay. He'd been led there by the vultures, which had almost picked the carcass clean.

He watered one horse—the other was blowing too hard—and while it drank, he walked over to the feeding frenzy and threw a couple of rocks at it.

"Get!" he cried. "Get out of here, you goddamn birds!"

When that didn't work, he ran toward them, shouting and flailing his arms.

The buzzards hopped off the corpse, but only strayed a few feet. They waited, their bald heads and beady eyes studying him greedily.

There wasn't anything to identify the dead horse as Lydia's, but a few minutes later, while the birds flocked back to cover the carcass again, he found a discarded saddlebag, tossed into the cactus.

Inside was a scrap of paper, probably the torn-off bottom of a receipt, yellowed with age. The edge of it read, ". . . otal $2.35," and under that, it read, ". . . ston West."

Goddamn Winston. The horse was hers all right.

Now, if he'd been her, where would he have gotten to?

He would have kept on going the same way, he figured. On toward those hills in the distance, and toward Cross Point, beyond.

She'd be on foot.

She'd be easy to find.

The bitch.

Billy Cree smiled to himself and mounted the fresher of the two horses. Leading the lathered mount, he started out at a jog, toward the east.

10

It would be dark very soon.

Lydia and Slocum had inventoried the food and water. They had enough to last them three days, if they were careful. But the baby? That was another thing. Little Tyler couldn't last that long.

She had fixed him another bottle of watered canned milk, and at the moment, he was drinking happily. She knew that he wasn't getting enough nourishment, but that would be all right if they could get him to civilization by say, tomorrow night. It didn't look like they would, though.

It made her sad beyond measure.

Slocum had lined up their water containers—three canteens and two half-full canvas bags—and set their food out in a row. Most of what he had needed cooking, since most of it was dried beans. But he had a few things that they could eat without preparation and without a fire: jerky and hardtack and a few unappetizing-looking carrots. A tin of canned peaches, too.

She wondered if she couldn't extend the baby's time with a little of that peach juice, and decided she'd try it. Maybe tonight.

Right now, all she could see of Slocum was his outline. He was toward the front of the cave, watching across the way for those two miscreants. He had not spoken, nor had she—save for cooing to the baby—for the last fifteen minutes.

Briefly, she closed her eyes and thought about his kiss.

A new wave of shivers overtook her spine. It had been better than two years since she'd felt that way, and she relished the feeling.

Winston surely had never left her in shivers, but when you were grateful to a man for pulling you out of perdition, you made allowances.

It struck her—again—that this Slocum must be some kind of lover.

She found herself wishing, and wishing hard, that when and if they got to town, he wouldn't go riding out anytime quick. She wanted him to stay around. She wanted to sample him, so to speak.

Tyler finished his bottle, and she rocked him up onto her shoulder.

I shouldn't be thinking about that, she scolded herself. *I should be thinking about this baby. I should be figuring out what to do next. If we get out of this alive, that is. And most of all, I shouldn't be thinking about a man.*

But try as she might, she couldn't help but think about Slocum. Just the outline of his shoulders against the darkening sky had her in a flutter.

"Just stop it," she whispered, beneath her breath. "Just stop it, you idiot!"

The baby burped—and spit up.

After lowering the child, Lydia wiped at her shoulder, muttering a soft, "Damn."

"If it's not one end, it's the other," Slocum said. He had turned his head, and was grinning at her.

She smiled back, glad that the fading sun meant neither of them could see the other clearly. She didn't need another blinding blast of his sex appeal right at the moment, and she also was grateful he hadn't seen her blush.

Or so she hoped.

"Babies are difficult," she said, and let the *at least, I guess so* remain unspoken. She decided to focus on a more immediate subject and said, "Do you think it's safe to light a fire?"

"No," he said.

"Oh."

She hadn't expected such an abrupt reply, but she simply nodded her head in acknowledgment.

Then he said, "Don't mean to be curt with you, honey. Sorry. I'm just tryin' to figure what those polecats'll be up to next."

He reached into his pocket, pulled out his smoking pouch, and started to roll himself a cigarette as he spoke. "Now," he went on, "they said they were gonna try to outlast us. Kind of like a siege in a war, I reckon. Wait till the fort runs out of food and water, then charge it and massacre the leftovers. Leftover people, I mean."

"I got that impression, too," Lydia said. She tucked the baby, who had fallen asleep, into the nest she had made for him from her blanket. "Come to any conclusions about what we should do?"

"Well," he said, licking his smoke and sticking it into his mouth, "they ain't gonna fight it out with us. Just as well, 'cause they got some mighty fine cover over there. Better than we've got."

He flicked a lucifer into life and held it to his smoke, drawing deeply. She loved a man who smoked. Winston had smoked a little corncob pipe, but that wasn't the same.

"They've also got at least one full water bag—that was on Ed's horse—plus whatever water and grub Charlie had on him. And unlike us, they're free to shoot game."

"And build a fire," Lydia groused.

"That, too," he said. "I don't figure they're too worried

about us gunnin' 'em or hightailin' it. After all, we've got
Tyler to worry about. Except that Tyler isn't gonna make
it any three days. He's the shortest on supplies of any of
us. So, if we're smart, we're gonna do one of two things.
Either try to sneak around and bushwhack 'em, or else
make a break for it tonight," he finished.

Despite herself, Lydia was startled by this. "Tonight?"
she said. "Won't they be watching?"

"Tonight. Unless you want to spend the next couple of
days knee-deep in horse shit," Slocum said with a grin. It
was perfectly timed, because just then Tubac lifted his tail
and let go.

Lydia looked at the fresh manure and said, "I see your
point." She turned back toward him. "When do we go?"

"Not yet," he said, and blew out a plume of smoke.
"Not till the dark, hard middle of the night. At least one
of them'll have to sleep. I'm hopin' it'll be Charlie."

"And what's to keep them from following us? If we
run, I mean."

"Nothin'," Slocum said with a shrug. "Nothin' at all."

Round about ten, Charlie walked softly toward where Ed
was keeping watch. Ed had a cozy nook. He was well
hidden by an outcrop that just happened to be cleft down
the middle, to a point above the ground where Ed could
sit comfortably with his eye to the bottom of the slit in
the rock. He had a clear view of the cave's mouth.

Charlie crouched down beside him. "Anything?" he
asked.

"Nope," replied Ed. "Just some shadows after we finished dinner, and now nothin'. They ain't lit a fire, leastwise, that I can tell."

"Slocum wouldn't," Charlie said.

Ed furrowed his brow. "Why not?"

Sometimes Ed could be just plain dense. "Because,"
Charlie said, "he's Slocum. He's smart and crafty. If you

was down there, would you light a big ol' fire so that every move you made would be lit up?"

Ed opened his mouth, but Charlie said, "Oh, I suppose you would. Well, Slocum ain't you and he ain't me. Why, we could'a shot him a half dozen times out there this afternoon, but we didn't. Why? 'Cause he was too damned quick for us, that's why! Practically blended in with the goddamn rocks."

Ed grinned at him. "Hey, Charlie, I bet even you didn't figure on him comin' out of that cave, six-guns blazin'!"

Charlie sighed. "Well, no, Ed, I didn't. And he didn't charge out, he snuck out. The guns came later. See, that's the trouble with a smart and wily man. He'll think of things that regular fellers don't."

"But you're smart, Charlie."

"Smart's kind of a relative thing, Ed," Charlie said. He was a tad annoyed that Ed was pursuing the subject so intently. "I may be smarter than you, but I may not be as smart as Slocum. That remains to be seen."

"Oh, we'll be seein' his remains, all right," Ed said, and brayed out a laugh.

Briefly, Charlie closed his eyes and held his tongue. Then he sighed and said, "You stay on watch for a while. Wake me up in a couple'a hours and I'll spell you."

Ed nodded. "Gotcha, Charlie."

Charlie turned on his heel and walked back toward their fire. Ed was a dolt, all right, but at least he was a dolt that Charlie could count on, one who'd never cross him. That was something, all right.

So as mad as Charlie got at times, he tried to hold his tongue and hold his punches. Not an easy feat for a man like him. But he knew that no matter what, Ed would not only stick by him, but take his orders so long as they lived.

Charlie was counting on that being a very long time.

Hopefully, in California. With a gold mine.

He lay down in his bedroll, pulled the blanket up to his chin, eased his hat low over his eyes, and fell asleep, happily assured of a soon-to-be-dead Slocum and his soon-to-be-realized riches.

Slocum had a change of plans.

The more he thought about it, he was thinking that he'd be better off sneaking up behind them. He figured that he had a pretty good chance of getting them both, but even if he only took down one, that'd be one less chasing them.

Besides, he had to get that baby to town—and to some real milk—as soon as possible.

So at around midnight, he took the dozing Lydia's shoulder and shook it gently.

She sat forward with a start and yelped, "What!"

"Shh!" Slocum hissed.

"Is it time to go?" she whispered.

"No," he said. "It's time for you to stand watch. Think you can do that?"

"Yes," she said, nodding. "Did you decide to sneak up on them? I thought we were just going to run away."

Slocum wished she hadn't quite put it that way, but he just said, "No. We'll hightail it later. I'm hopin' I can take both of them out, though."

She nodded. "What do you want me to do?" she asked. She had guts, this one. Most women would have been cowering in the back of the cave from the moment they dived into it, and they'd still be back there, crying and shaking.

"Just like you did this afternoon," he said. "Take the rifle and watch the front door." He jabbed a finger toward the mouth of the cave. "You see anybody coming that ain't me, you fire."

"All right," she said.

"You a pretty fair shot?"

"I can knock a can off a fence post at forty feet," she replied.

"Okay. Just think of that fella chargin' down on you like he's a tin of stewed tomatoes."

A soft chuckle escaped her, and she held out a hand for the rifle. "Got it. Tomatoes. I never did like stewed tomatoes."

"That's my girl," he said without thinking, and to his surprise, she blushed. At least, he thought she did. There wasn't much moon filtering into the cave.

He handed over the rifle. He said, "Be ready."

"Good luck, Slocum," she whispered, and quickly leaned forward and kissed his cheek.

He was surprised, but got over it quick. He murmured, "I'm gonna need more luck than that, honey," he said, and kissed her deeply.

11

Slocum moved slowly and quietly, creeping from boulder to rocky scatter to stunted creosote bush or palo verde. He'd seen the glow from their fire all night. They hadn't bothered to hide it, the idiots. Unless, of course, they'd set up camp somewhere else and had lit the fire as a decoy.

But he didn't think they were that smart. At least, he hoped they weren't.

He worked his way down the canyon almost to the point where they'd been ambushed that afternoon, a place where he'd seen what looked like a way up. He figured it was where Charlie had come down from the pass's rim to its floor. If Charlie could come down it on a horse, he could go up it on foot.

He wanted to get up above them. It was the safest way.

Carefully, he crossed out into the moonlit, unshadowed open. Nobody shot at him, thank God, so they weren't watching this part of the pass.

And apparently, they hadn't seen him sneaking out, either.

But you never could tell.

He began to make his way up the rough trail. Part of

it, he could almost walk. Other parts, he went down on his hands and knees and pulled himself along with his bad shoulder, painfully zigzagging ever upward.

He was panting by the time he reached the rim, and thankful that the canyon hadn't been any deeper than it was.

He sat for a moment on the rim, catching his breath and scouting the terrain. He could still see the faint glow of Ed and Charlie's fire, flaring up along the undulating rim. But when he started moving again, he was still on his guard. He moved slowly and carefully, and as silently as possible.

Finally, he got down on his belly and crawled, crawled, and crawled some more, right back up to the rim, just to the side of the glow from their campfire, below. Silently, he sank down onto his belly.

One was asleep under his blanket, almost straight down from Slocum's perch, back beside their fire. The other one was out about twenty feet, hunkered up against a split jut of rock. There was a rifle across his knees, and he was snoring.

Well, that accounts for nobody seein' me, Slocum thought. He was annoyed at that boy—he thought it was Ed—just on general principle. And then he wondered why he was peeved with Ed, when Ed's actions had made his task so much easier. Maybe it was the rock poking into his belly.

It sort of bothered Slocum to take out two sleeping men, but he didn't see that he had much choice. Of course, he could just wound them. But then, he'd have to wound them good enough to slow them down a whole lot.

He shook his head. *All right,* he thought. *I'll aim for the legs. But the chips are gonna fall where they will.*

He raised his gun and aimed for the sentry, Ed, first.

He fired, and as Ed let out a yelp, he aimed almost straight down, into the dozing figure under the blankets.

The blanket jerked at the impact, but that was all.

Ed, his gun dropped in favor of clutching his thigh, started screaming, "Charlie! Charlie! I'm shot, damn it!"

Slocum figured that Charlie wasn't going to answer, since Charlie appeared to be dead. But then again, how could a slug entering the blankets right about knee level kill a man? And why wasn't there any blood?

Hissing, "Shit !" through clenched teeth, Slocum realized there was nobody under those blankets to get shot. They were probably packed with clothes and an extra bedroll.

Which meant that Charlie could be anywhere.

The too-close sound of a pistol's cock told him where.

He froze.

"I don't believe it," Charlie said, before he shouted, "Shut up, dammit!" to his brother. "Me, little ol' Charlie Frame, gettin' the drop on Mr. Big Famous Slocum hisself!"

Slocum couldn't believe it either, but he turned his head upward, toward the voice. "Congratulations," he said sarcastically.

Charlie had a great big grin splitting his face. "You gonna put that gun down, or you want I should just shoot it out of your hand?"

Slowly, Slocum lay down his Colt.

"Charlie!" Ed cried. "I'm bleedin' awful bad!"

"Just hold your horses, dammit," Charlie called back. "I got me a real true legend of the West in my gun sights. Let me enjoy it for a minute!"

Slocum was still flat on his belly, and he was trying to figure a way to swing his body over, move just one foot closer to Charlie. Twelve inches closer, give or take, and he'd be able to knock Charlie's feet out from under him with a quick sweep of his leg. Then they'd see who was in goddamn charge!

Carefully, he gathered a handful of grit and dust from the ground. Best to have a backup.

He was just about to fling it, to hopefully blind Charlie long enough to move those lousy twelve inches, when a shot rang out from below.

Charlie, surprise twisting his face, staggered back, then sat down hard, which gave Slocum the second he needed to drop the dirt and grab his Colt.

Charlie had fumbled his pistol on the way down, and Slocum went over, in a crouch, and kicked it out about ten feet. Charlie was gasping like a fish that had been pulled up on the docks.

"You shot me, you sonofabitch!" Charlie managed to spit out. "How'd you do that?"

Slocum shook his head. "I didn't shoot you." A trace of a smile spread over his lips, and he had no inclination to pull it back. "My partner did. Now, I got half a mind to plug you where you lay, Charlie. But I was cogitatin' on lettin' you boys live. And I reckon that it wouldn't be real sportsmanlike, lead-nailing your coffin while you're all helpless and everything."

Slocum walked out to where he'd kicked Charlie's gun, and picked it up. He emptied the chambers, threw the cartridges as far as he could to his left, then threw the Smith and Wesson as far as he could to his right.

"Reckon that'll settle your hash for the time bein'," he said.

"I'm bleedin' to death!" Charlie wailed.

Slocum sat down. "Aw, no you ain't. I seen a lot worse. I seen men hurt worse than you get right up and pick up the charge, back in the War. Now, what in the world did you no-accounts want with that poor little baby?"

Charlie set his mouth and turned his head away. Blood seeped slowly through his fingers, which were clasped to his wounded shoulder.

Slocum's put his Colt's nose to Charlie's kneecap and cocked it. That got his attention.

"Hey!" Charlie shouted in surprise and fear. "What the hell you doin'?"

"Believe I'm getting ready to shoot your kneecap off, there, Charlie, unless you tell me what the deal is with that kid."

Charlie's Adam's apple bobbed up and down. He blinked twice. "You wouldn't," he said.

"Push me," said Slocum.

Charlie wasn't as dumb as he looked. He said, "All right! Just move that gun away!"

Slocum didn't budge.

"It's the gold mine, all right? The kid's pa wandered into our camp, talked all about it. We want the kid 'cause we want the gold." Charlie, who had seemingly exhausted himself with this confession, let his head flop back onto the ground.

But Slocum wasn't done yet. "What happened to the kid's pa?" he asked.

"Dead," said Charlie. He turned his head away. "It was an accident, all right?"

Slocum didn't believe him, not by a long shot, but what was done was done. He had half a mind to shoot the bastard in the other shoulder, though, just on general principle.

But he didn't.

Instead, he eased down the hammer of his gun, then scrambled back over to the canyon's rim. Ed was still down there. He hadn't moved a foot.

"Ed!" Slocum called.

Ed looked up and squinted, trying to see into the gloom. "Slocum? You ain't dead?"

"Not yet, Ed," Slocum called.

"What about Charlie?"

"He's a little shot up, but other than that he's dandy," Slocum answered. "Ed?"

"Yeah?"

"Why don't you toss that rifle of yours up over that big rock you're sittin' against?" It wasn't a question, really.

And Ed didn't take it as one. He heaved that rifle as hard as he could, and Slocum heard the rattle when it hit the ground on the other side.

"That's right nice, Ed," Slocum called. "You got a side arm that's wantin' to join it?"

Slocum watched as Ed sighed, then pulled his gun free of its holster. The gun sparkled blue and silver in the campfire's light as it went up and over the rock.

"That's a good feller, Ed," Slocum said. Then he shouted, "Lydia! You hear me?"

Her answer came to him, carried on the canyon air currents: "I hear you! We're all packed up and ready to go!"

God, the woman was a miracle! And a mind reader, too!

"Come on out, baby, toward the fire!" he called. "You can walk right into their camp. I want you to snag their horses!"

"Our horses?" Charlie and Ed shouted as one. Charlie was plain outraged, but Ed appeared to be more shocked than anything.

"You heard me," Slocum growled at Charlie.

In answer, Lydia shouted one word, "Right!"

"You can't take a man's horse," Charlie complained.

"Seems to me I can do just about anything I want, Charlie," Slocum said with a grin. He called down to Ed, "Tie your leg off with your bandana, Ed. Above the bullet hole. It'll slow down the bleedin'."

Ed shouted back, "Thanks, Slocum!" He didn't look all that grateful, though.

Slocum still didn't like him, not one whit, but just because you didn't care to keep a man's company didn't mean you should let him bleed to death.

Just then, Lydia peeked around the big cleft rock, and Slocum called, "It's okay. Come ahead."

He watched as she walked out into the sheltered clearing Ed and Charlie had chosen for their hideaway, and waved down at her. She answered with a tip of her head and a big grin.

Once she'd snagged the horses and saddled them up, Slocum called down, "Leave 'em enough water so they can walk into town. Go on ahead and start down the pass, toward Cross Point. I'll meet you farther down the canyon."

He waited until she led the horses past the rock, out of the light. Then, shaking his head, Slocum backed away from the rim, backed away from the prostrate Charlie, and disappeared into the shadows.

Charlie shouted, "Coward!" just once.

Slocum didn't know whether that remark was meant for him or for Ed. Frankly, he didn't much care.

He jogged back to the canyon rim till he came to the trail that led downward. Holding out his arms for balance, he started to skitter down the slope toward the canyon's floor.

It was dangerous going. In fact, he slipped and nearly broke his neck on one occasion. But all in all, it was a lot easier than going up had been.

He heard, then saw Lydia emerge from the shadows: the baby in her arms and the three horses, tied in a line and trailing behind her.

Slocum smiled.

12

Billy Cree hadn't stopped at nightfall, mostly because just as the sun was going down, he'd found the place where the Kid's bitch had met up with somebody. Now she had a ride again, goddamn it, and he had to hurry if he wanted to catch them before they made Cross Point.

But the tracks were so clear and fresh that even by the light of the moon and stars, he could follow them fairly easily.

Mostly, he rode at a jog. He switched horses when necessary, and only stopped when he had trailed them clean across that broad expanse and come to the base of the hills.

He finally made camp at ten o'clock at night, there at the beginning of the rise of hills. He figured that the track would be too easy to lose as it wound through their crests and valleys. And the horses were all worn out.

Not that he really cared, but he had to keep the horses in halfway decent condition if he wanted to keep on Lydia's trail.

He'd show her a thing or two before he finished her off, too!

Damned murdering bitch!

He'd almost missed the place where they picked up the second rider. In fact, he'd suddenly realized that he was trailing two horses instead of one, and had to backtrack to see where the tracks joined up.

It looked to him like a chance encounter: two parties running into each other smack dab in the middle of nowhere. Such things were known to happen. But still, it set the back of his neck to itching.

His trigger finger, too. Lydia might have two men with her now. Two guns to protect her. It was a good deal different from going up against an unarmed woman on her own.

But crisp, clear thinking had never been Billy Cree's strong suit. He had always been more like a short, red-headed terrier with a bone: Once he got his jaws—or mind—wrapped around something, it was almost impossible to make him let go.

Like tracking the Kid, for instance.

Up until three years ago, the Show Low Kid and Billy Cree had been partners. Best friends, in fact, or so thought Billy. And then, one morning Billy woke up to find the Kid gone and the payroll they'd taken off the Flagstaff stage gone with him: over seven thousand dollars.

And so Billy figured he knew just what the price of friendship was to the Kid.

Well, he'd show the Kid.

It had taken him three years, but he'd done it.

Of course, he hadn't found the money. When he wasn't riding the Kid's woman, he'd been tearing up the house, tearing up the barn, going through the Kid's papers.

And no sign of it. It made him all the more ill-tempered toward that goddamn skirt. She didn't know anything. He was sure of that. She hadn't even known the true identity of her husband, Winston West—alias the Show Low Kid, alias Robert Craig Winston, born in the slums of Pittsburgh, Pennsylvania, and the son of a sometime store clerk and full-time drunk.

Hell, maybe he just gambled it away. He'd always been a sucker for an inside straight, and he'd never, not in all the years that Billy had known him, been seen to fill one.

'Course, it wasn't real romantic. But then, neither was Winston West. Billy supposed that the Kid had just tried to take a step partway back, to somewhere between wanted outlaw and town souse.

Which would have been fine, Billy supposed, if the Kid hadn't tried to step back with Billy's money.

Thirty-five hundred of that haul was supposed to be Billy's, and if Billy couldn't find it, he figured to take it out in trade. He hadn't ridden the Kid's woman near enough to feel even halfway paid off, though. And then she'd shot Randy and Wes, just like that!

A gut full of gall, that's what that woman had. Standing there in the doorway, plumb naked, with the pistols in her hands.

His boys had dropped like flies. Hadn't known what hit 'em.

Well, he had, too. And he still had the headache to show for it. Hell, he was lucky that he hadn't bled to death. He figured that he'd come close. He still felt a little weak, even though he'd patched his head and rested until the storm played out and fed himself decent, for a change.

So he settled the horses—his pinto and Randy's bay—ate the last of the roasted chicken, rolled himself up in a blanket, and fell into a fitful sleep.

Until a little after midnight, that was.

He woke to hear a short series of faint pops, like firecrackers on Independence Day, except way off somewhere in the hills. By the time he came fully awake, he realized it wasn't kids having a good time: It was gunplay.

Had Lydia's savior and the rider that had joined them

had a falling-out? Or had Lydia shot the both of them? He wouldn't put it past her.

He sat there a long time, staring and watching the hills, but there were no more shots, and he was too far away to see if there were any campfires.

"Goddamn it!" he muttered. "I sure hope they didn't kill that Lydia. I ain't through with her yet."

Despite all his griping about her, he had to admit one thing: She had the finest pair of tits he had ever seen.

He'd like to get his hands on them a few more times before he killed her.

"Goddamn it, Charlie!" Ed moaned. "Hurry up! Hurry up and help me fix my leg!" He had a bandana tied around his thigh, but it wasn't helping much.

He stared up into the rocky face of the canyon wall, where he'd seen Charlie's shadow struggle to its feet only moments before. But now it had disappeared again.

"Charlie!" Ed shouted. "You all right?"

Charlie didn't answer.

"Charlie, I'm gonna bleed to death, for the love'a Mike!"

At last, Charlie came into sight, sliding down the last few feet of the canyon wall on an angle, his hand plastered to his hurt shoulder, blood seeping through his fingers.

"Charlie!" Ed cried gleefully. "I thought you was dead!"

"You're gonna be dead if you don't stop hollerin' your fool head off," Charlie growled back at him. "Took me a while to find my gun. Didn't even try for the cartridges."

Ed cocked his head, puzzled. "Huh?"

"Never mind." Carefully, Charlie bent to the ground and picked up a small stick. He tossed it to Ed. "Put that though the bandana, then give her a turn."

Ed complied, and let out a yelp when he twisted the stick.

"Not that tight, you idiot," said Charlie with a disgusted shake of his head. "It's to slow up the bleedin', not take your stupid leg off."

Ed loosened the tourniquet just a tad, and relaxed a bit when he noticed that his blood wasn't soaking into the ground nearly as fast as it had been.

"Charlie?" he asked.

Charlie had plopped down beside the fire, and was presently staring at his own shoulder. "What?" he asked without looking up.

"How come you s'pose that Slocum didn't just kill us? I mean, he sure could have. Could have done it real easy."

"He's the type," Charlie mumbled, then grimaced. " 'Course, he's probably killed us, anyway. No horses and all. The bastard." He looked at his shoulder and scowled at it, as if to scare the wound away, Ed thought.

Charlie muttered, "Damned slug went all the way through."

"What you mean, he's the type?"

Charlie proceeded to take off his shirt, slosh water over his shoulder, then rip the shirt up into strips. The clean parts, anyway. Relatively speaking.

"I mean," he said, through the shirt fabric gripped in his teeth, "that he's just the type not to do it and get it over with. Got one of them Sir Galahad complexes or somethin'."

"Sir who?"

That Charlie! He was always going on about things that left Ed dangling in the wind.

"Never mind," grumped Charlie. "Sir somebody, anyhow." His bare chest looked ghostly white as he started winding the dirty fabric around his arm and over his shoulder. "That sonofabitch not only got our broomtails, he got my goddamn gun arm. It figures. It just figures."

"Charlie?" Ed tried again, attempting to look pitiful. "You gonna fix my leg?"

"Can't you fix it yourself, you turd bucket?"

Now, that sort of got Ed a little hot under the collar. Why, Charlie hadn't called him that since they were about six or seven! Of course, he thought, softening, it might had been a term of whatchacall . . . endearment.

He decided to give Charlie the benefit of the doubt and said, "Well, I don't rightly know how to start, Charlie."

Charlie sighed visibly, and tied off his own bandage. He turned toward his brother. "Is it broke? Slug hit the bone?"

Ed replied, "Don't think so."

"Did it come out the other side?"

Ed peered close, squinting, and ran his fingers along the inside of his leg. To be truthful, it was getting a little numb. He felt a tear in the fabric, and blood came away on his fingers. He looked up. "Yeah."

"Then you're a lucky man, Ed," Charlie said. "I don't gotta dig for the slug. And the way I'm feelin' right now, I can guarantee you it would'a been real painful."

Ed swallowed hard.

Charlie looked at his leg, and the tightness with which Ed was gripping the tourniquet, and said, "I reckon we need to pack the damned thing. And Ed, loosen up on that stick from time to time, all right? You cut off the circulation long enough, you'll lose the sonofabitching leg."

Slocum, mounted on Tubac, and Lydia and the baby, mounted on Charlie's purloined horse, had made reasonably good time down the canyon. In fact, they had left it behind and were currently twisting and winding their way blindly through and around a series of hills.

Slocum was about to give it up for the night. It was too hard to see where they were going, for one thing. He'd nearly ridden smack into a thicket of prickly pear a while back. Lydia, bless her heart, hadn't said a word about it.

It was a good woman who knew when to hold her tongue.

Besides, he figured they wouldn't see Charlie and Ed again.

He said, "We'll stop and make camp as soon as I spot a good place."

Lydia, who had been for the most part silent since they left the canyon, said, "Is that safe?" She looked back over her shoulder, then at Slocum.

"They're not comin'," he said. "At least, not tonight. They ain't got any horses, for one thing. Ed's shot in the leg pretty bad, and you shot Charlie in his gun arm." He paused. You must'a been some kind of can-shooter," he said with a smile.

"That's me," she said. "World champion can killer." He couldn't see her face clearly, but there was a smile in the words.

"Well," he allowed, "likely, those two numbskulls will forget all about us and drag into town in their own good time. If the Lord's smilin' on us, that'll be about a week after we leave."

Lydia nodded slowly. "You don't think a gold mine is worth a little pain on the trail? That they wouldn't do anything to get it? And the baby?"

"Nope," Slocum said.

He figured them for cowards at heart, and cowardly men seldom went out of their way for much of anything. Especially when going out of their way meant they'd have to endure a great deal of physical pain. And a probable death—at his hands—even if they lived through the trek.

He spotted a cavity in the rock ahead, and pointed. "That look like a cave to you?"

Lydia shrugged.

"Well, it looks like one to me," Slocum stated. "I believe we should check it out. If there ain't any bats and a mountain lion's not makin' it his lair, I'm all for holin' up for the night."

Lydia rode up next to him. "You check it over," she said with just a hint of a smile. Lord, she was pretty by the moonlight, once a fellow could see her! "I'll hold the baby."

"That'd be right helpful, ma'am," Slocum said, grinning. Hell, she hadn't taken a hand off that baby since back in the canyon.

They reined in their horses outside the cave and Slocum dismounted. He handed Lydia Tubac's reins and those of Ed's mount, drew his gun, popped a lucifer into flame, and entered the cave.

13

There were, indeed, no bats in residence. Nor was there any evidence that any had ever inhabited the small cave. The ceiling wasn't high enough to accommodate the horses, but there was a small sheltered spot just outside. They'd be fine.

He walked back to Lydia and took the baby from her arms for a moment so that she could dismount, and then he led the horses to the place he'd picked out for them. Lydia followed.

"You can go on inside," he said as he loosened Tubac's girth, then pulled the saddle from his back.

She arched a brow and cocked her head. "Not on your life," she replied as he set the saddle away from the horses. "Not until you get a fire going in there. I'm not taking the chance that I'll lay little Tyler on a scorpion. Or a sleeping rattlesnake. Or a black widow, for that matter."

Slocum smiled. "All right, then. But I'm gonna settle these horses first."

"How many miles do you think we've come since we left them?" she asked.

"Ed and Charlie? Maybe five miles. Hard to tell in

103

these hills. They're like a maze. But I can guarantee you
that they're still sitting around that fire of theirs, gripin'
up a storm and tryin' to find somethin' to bandage their
wounds and cursin' my name. Probably my whole family,
too."

Lydia snorted. "I'd bet cash money on that last part,"
she said with a grin. The baby was fussing, and she rocked
him in her arms.

To Slocum, she said, "We're almost out of milk. I
think there's only enough left for one feeding. You've got
a can of peaches, though. Might I try the peach syrup?
It'd fill his tummy, at least. And the sugar's better for him
than just water."

"Don't see why not," Slocum replied.

He had unsaddled all three horses, exchanged bridles
for halters, and was in the process of rationing out oats
for each mount. He was thinking that it was a good thing
they'd make Cross Point tomorrow. Tubac's oats
wouldn't stretch for three very long, and there was so little
fodder out here for grazing that he figured you couldn't
even count it.

He bent and picked up his saddlebags, unbuckled one
side, and rummaged around until his hand found the tin
of peaches.

"Hang on to this for a second," he said, "and I'll get
you a fire started in the cave."

"Thanks."

He paused, then said, "I hope somebody's told you
how pretty you are. Somebody ought to tell you that. All
the time."

He believed she blushed. He knew that he, himself,
came close to it. He hadn't quite expected to say that.

She quickly ducked her head, and despite her stated
misgivings about the cave, carried the baby inside. Slocum could see just the edge of her skirt as she waited
inside the mouth.

Smiling oddly, he began to gather up some kindling and firewood.

It gave Lydia a bit of a start when he appeared out of nowhere, a bundle of sticks under one arm.

"Oh!" she said. "It's you!"

"You were expecting somebody else?" he said.

She couldn't see his face, as he had squatted down on his heels farther back in the cave, and was arranging the wood. Or so she thought. The inside of the cave was as black as the innards of a black sow, and she couldn't see a blasted thing. But there was a hint of a chuckle in his voice.

"No," she said, and sighed. The baby was still fussing, a little worse all the time, and she knew it was only a matter of time until he erupted into full-blown wails.

She couldn't say that she blamed him. He had to be terribly hungry. Babies, she'd been told, had very small stomachs and very big appetites. In just her short experience, she believed it.

Slocum flicked a match. The glow of it faintly outlined his figure as he squatted before the fire and bent to blow life into the kindling. Lydia could hear the snap and pop of dead grasses bursting into flame, and before long, the sticks and branches took. Light washed up, a flickering gold, over the interior of the little cave.

She looked around for snakes and scorpions and the like, and deeming it safe, took a few steps closer to the fire and sat down. Tyler was beginning to squall, and she held up the tin, saying, "Hush, little one. Yummy peach juice is coming."

Slocum stood up. God, he was handsome. Despite everything, she wanted him more and more. She wondered how on earth she could tell him she wanted him, or coax him into seducing her, or . . .

"I'll get his bottle and the rest of his gear," Slocum said.

He ducked out of the cave and disappeared into the night.

Slocum didn't know what the hell to think.

He crammed their bedrolls under his arm and slung their saddlebags over his shoulder with a bemused expression. It seemed like she was interested. As interested as he was.

But she'd been through a whole heap of trouble these last days, and it was the kind of trouble that was about the worst and lowest to perpetrate on a woman. He sure didn't want to press himself on her if she wasn't up to it. He thought too much of her to do that.

But then, she plain might not be interested in him at all.

"Well, what the hell," Slocum muttered as he grabbed one of the water bags along with the possibles bag, holding them by their necks in one big fist. "You can't win if you don't play."

His mind set, his hands and arms full, he started back toward the cave and its glowing mouth.

Lydia noticed a new resolve in him when he came back, but she set herself to the business of feeding the baby. Slocum pried open the tin of peaches with a pocketknife, and she carefully poured some of the syrup into Tyler's bottle, then topped it off with water. It was too thick for the baby and too thick for the nipple, and she thought that a sudden surge of all the sugar might not be the best thing for him. At least, it never did her any good.

Tyler seemed to like it quite a bit. At least, he stopped squalling the moment she held the nipple to his lips, and suckled it enthusiastically. So enthusiastically, in fact, that she had to take it away for a few seconds to let the baby catch his breath.

Across the little fire, Slocum was preparing their meal: coffee, biscuits, gravy, period. Once again, they had no meat. Of course, that wasn't Slocum's fault. It was those damned brothers. Maybe tomorrow Slocum would shoot a jackrabbit. No, scratch that. Tomorrow, they'd be in town.

This last thought was accompanied by a sigh of relief that came from her, unbidden, and Slocum looked up from his labors.

"What?" he said.

"I was just thinking. Tomorrow we'll be safe in town."

He nodded, and set the biscuits on to bake. "I could sure use a steak."

She grinned. "I'll buy you one. It's the least I can do to say thank you." And then, realizing that there was actually quite a bit more she could do—and wanted to do— she blushed.

He didn't say anything, but he must have known what was on her mind. He gave her a funny little grin that went all the way from his mouth to his eyes and back—and half-intoxicated her—before he turned toward the bubbling gravy.

My Lord, she thought. *My dear, sweet Lord!*

She got past it though, past the sudden surge of warmth she felt between her legs, and got back to the more pressing business of tending the baby. By the time he was fed and his diapers changed and he had fallen asleep and been put down on a nest of saddle blankets, Slocum had dished out the supper.

She took her plate gratefully. She ate, in fact, like a starving woman and washed the biscuits and gravy down with good, hot coffee. And by the time she had dredged the last fork full of biscuit in the last of the gravy and swallowed it, she suddenly realized that Slocum was no longer across the fire. He had moved beside her, sitting so close that he was almost touching her.

Again, that warm, wet, glowing feeling started in her crotch and spread out over her body.

She didn't say anything. She simply set her plate and cup aside, turned her face toward his, and placed her hand lightly on the back of his neck.

"You sure?" he murmured, a touch of worry underscoring his words.

"Yes," she said.

He bent and kissed her: tenderly, sweetly, at first, and then the kiss blossomed, grew, became deeper, and suddenly she was lost in it, completely lost.

She didn't know how, but she became aware that she was lying down, still kissing him, still reveling in it, and that her clothes were gone. She supposed she had helped to take them off, but didn't remember it. All she remembered was his kiss, his touch, his scent.

His hands were everywhere, caressing her, stroking her: her breasts, her arms, her stomach, her hips, her throat, everywhere. And he was naked, too. The hard muscles of his arms and back felt strong, animal-like, but controlled.

She opened her legs to him, and he needed no further invitation. He entered her slowly at first, slipping in his massive girth easily as she stretched to accommodate him, and she sighed deeply at the sensation, the ecstatic sensation of feeling full, and the promise of feeling complete.

But she wasn't complete yet.

Gently, he began to move inside her, rocking, sliding, gradually picking up his pace. Her knees rose to hug his sides, and she imagined that they were the flanks of a wild animal, a voracious wild beast who was tender only with his mate.

He moved atop her, kissing her lips, her throat, her ears, lapping at her breasts, filling her with sensations she hadn't felt in years—if indeed, she'd ever felt them at all. And she hadn't. Not like this.

And she felt a fire burning between her legs, a fire that she knew would soon burst into a bright and blinding flame.

She clung to him, this beautiful man. She rose to meet his every thrust. She began to lose herself even more, began to give herself over to the moment, to the second, to nothing but sensation.

And then it rose up in her, the overwhelming moment, the one she wished would go on and on, last forever. She rose and rose, as if she were flying though a cloud of pure sensation, pure ecstacy, pure bliss, until she exploded into a shattering orgasm.

She felt a cry come from her throat. What she called out, she wasn't sure. She was too lost in pleasure.

She felt the power as Slocum rammed into her twice more, felt his shudder as he spilled his seed deep within her, and then felt the weight of his body as he sagged down upon her.

He kissed her lips again, even as she felt her internal muscles contracting, releasing, contracting, releasing, hugging him tight, from the intensity and might of her orgasm.

Against his lips, she whispered, "My God, Slocum. Thank you." She knew then that he was exactly what she had needed in this time and this place, exactly what she had needed to make sense of her life again. "Thank you so very much."

And before he had a chance to reply, she kissed him.

14

Charlie and Ed Frame rose early the next morning. Well, Charlie, anyway. Ed hadn't slept a wink. He'd been concentrating on the fierce pain in his leg all night, and it was still pounding as they gathered up what was left of their possessions and started east, toward Cross Point. At least it wasn't bleeding anymore. That was, until he stood up and let go of it long enough to take a lengthy piss.

A rough-hewn crutch made of hastily whittled palo verde under his arm, Ed joined Charlie again. Squinting against the sun, he said, "Don't see what the goldurn rush is. I'm bleedin' again. And they're long gone, Charlie."

"Maybe, maybe not," replied his brother. He was just finishing up loading their water, bedrolls, and saddlebags onto a crudely made travois. "Just twist that thing tighter."

Ed hoped Charlie intended to lug that travois. He knew he was in no condition. Hell, he was afraid he'd fall down with every faltering step he took!

Thankfully, Charlie tied down the last of their belongings, then stepped between the traces. Ed relaxed a little.

"Well?" asked Charlie, in that accusatory tone Ed loathed.

"Well, what?"

Charlie rolled his eye skyward. "You comin' or not, gimp?"

Ed frowned. "Soon's you start out, Mr. Shot-Through-the-Shoulder, I'll follow."

Charlie muttered "Jesus" beneath his breath, and started forward, dragging the travois behind him.

Slocum's trail was easy to follow, even for two crippled low-life criminals on foot. And, Ed reminded himself, they were following their own stolen horses. Maybe that helped.

Although Charlie had packed Ed's leg wounds and bandaged them up tight last night, when Charlie got to pulling that travois too fast—and Ed had to hobble double-time just to keep up—it got to oozing and seeping worse than ever, and Ed got a touch more worried.

"Charlie?" he said.

Charlie didn't look back. He didn't have to. His arm wasn't bleeding at all this morning.

"Charlie!" he repeated, more plaintively this time.

"What!" Charlie snapped.

"Charlie, my leg's bleedin' a bit. Mayhap we could slow down some. Or take us a rest."

Still, Charlie didn't look back. Or stop. He simply said, "You lunatic! We only been walkin' ten minutes. You want me to shoot you right here like a lame horse? I could make a lot better time, you know."

Ed didn't need to think about this too much, and he said, "No, I guess I don't."

"Don't what?"

"Don't want you should shoot me. But I don't like to think about bleedin' to death, neither."

Charlie finally stopped, and for a minute Ed was a little scared that maybe Charlie was going to pull that Smith & Wesson and shoot him in the head. Put him out of his misery, so to speak.

Except he didn't want to be put out of his misery, he just wanted Charlie to slow the hell down!

But Charlie didn't go for his gun. Looking awful cranky, he snapped, "Just take that bandana off'n your neck again and tie it round your leg. Get you a stick. Hell," he added with a grumbling growl, "I'll go fetch one. You'll take all damned day."

Charlie bent down until his eye fell on part of a branch, and he tossed it to Ed, who missed it. It bounced off his chest and fell at his feet.

"Make a tourniquet, like last night," Charlie went on. "I'll give you a couple'a minutes. But not more." He crossed his arms over his chest and began to tap his toe. "Snap it up, Eddie."

"I'm snappin', dammit, I'm snappin'," Ed grumbled as he slid the bandana off his neck and tied it around his thigh.

While Ed and Charlie Frame were grumbling over tourniquets, Billy Cree was well on his way toward them.

He had risen before dawn, and was in the saddle when the sun was just peeking over the horizon. It was enough light to trail by, he reasoned, and that was all he needed.

His hat pulled low over his eyes against the rising sun, he had followed the trail up into the hills and their maze. And now, after just two hours of up and down and looping around, he came upon the site of a bonafide ruckus.

He dismounted and followed the tracks all around, trying to make sense of them.

Now, Billy Cree was a pretty fair tracker, even if he did say so himself. And he did. Often. It didn't take him very long to discern that there had been an ambush, and that one of the riders—the newest one that Lydia had picked up—hadn't been a part of it.

It looked like this new boy'd had a partner up on top of the canyon, too. Lydia and the other fellow had galloped back up the canyon, retracing their steps, and skittered into a cave, which proved to have been used, but was now deserted.

Also, it looked like the man had tried to make a run for it on foot. Fresh bullet marks scarred the canyon walls, peppered them. The man had made it back inside, though. Tracks didn't lie.

Neither did the blood that Billy found spattered on the rocks and inside the cave.

But the man must not have been hurt too bad. He'd come out again later. He'd followed the wall of the canyon, then cut across and gone up.

Must have been quite a show up there, from what Billy could tell. There was blood all over the place, for one thing, and more down below, where it looked like the ambushers had made camp. He found the remains of a fire, at least, when he went down. He also found the signs of bedrolls having been laid out and lots of feet stomping around.

Whoever this galoot was that Lydia had hooked up with, he was a tough bird. It appeared to Billy that he'd bested his attackers—hadn't killed them though, which sort of puzzled Billy—and he'd made off with their horses.

At least he had found Lydia's tiny boot prints there in their camp, half hidden by the ambushers' big footprints, and Lydia had led their horses away.

Billy worked his way out of the rocks that had sheltered the ambushers, walked back to his horse, and pushed back his hat. Damn! This was surely a puzzlement! He knew why *he* was after Lydia, but why the hell would those other fellas be after her?

On the other hand, maybe they were after her traveling companion.

Billy snorted. By the looks of it, it'd take more than the two of those yahoos to take this tough old pelican out.

He seemed to have made goddamn fools out of them last night.

He mounted up, saddle leather complaining. And straightened out the lead rope on the spare horse. Well, maybe the two bushwhackers couldn't handle this fellow of Lydia's, but then, they weren't Billy Cree, were they? He figured to find out just who they were in a matter of perhaps an hour, an hour and a half: They had set out on foot.

One was dragging a travois behind him, and one was walking with a crutch. He was still losing blood, too. There was a little trickle of it every now and then, turning the dust and gravel rust-colored. They wouldn't be making very good time.

And their tracks were fresh, almost brand-new. They were on top of the horses' tracks, and he knew that Lydia was on one of those horses.

He jogged along, following the trail with ease. And he thought that it would sure be nice if those yahoos didn't turn out to be such yahoos after all. Maybe they'd be lucky enough to catch up to Lydia and her man and kill him. After all, he was only interested in Lydia.

That murdering bitch.

Slocum and Lydia had gotten an early start, too, although they were somewhat the worse for wear for not having had much sleep the night before. However, Slocum thought that Lydia looked, well, all glowy. She couldn't seem to keep from smiling.

And frankly, neither could he. He'd be glad to get into Cross Point—which he figured to do around mid-afternoon—turn in the baby, have himself a bath, then settle down in a nice hotel bed with Lydia.

By the looks of it, he didn't imagine her complaining.

They were still leading the spare horse. Well, Slocum was leading him, anyway. He trailed along behind Tubac, his head down, his ribs showing through his dull coat. The one Lydia was riding wasn't much better looking. It seemed those Frame boys had been down on their luck for quite some time.

Well, Slocum would have to be a whole lot more beat up and beat back before he'd ever let a horse of his get into that state! When they got into town, he was going to put those Frame horses at the livery on full grain feed for a few days. That ought to put a little spark back in their eyes, all right.

Might shine up those old coats a tad, too.

"What time is it?"

He looked over at Lydia, who was still smiling softly. He returned the expression, then checked his pocket watch.

" 'Bout eleven," he said. "Ten-to, to be exact about it. Why? You got a hot date waitin' in town?"

She pursed her lips in a mock reprimand, but her eyes were still smiling. "As a matter of fact, I do have myself a date with a beau. But he won't arrive until I do."

Slocum reached over and cupped a wide hand around her thigh. "Just exactly when you do, Lydia." Then he pulled back, rested his hand on the saddle horn, and asked, "How's Tyler doin' today?"

The thinned-down peach juice had held him for a while last night, but she'd had to give him more of it, more frequently, than she had the milk.

"We've only got enough milk left for one watery feeding," she said. "Thank God we're nearly there. About three, you think?"

He nodded. "Or thereabouts."

"I hope we can find him a wet nurse," she went on. "Breast milk is what he really needs."

Slocum almost commented that it didn't sound too bad to him, either, but withheld the remark. Things were going pretty good with Lydia right at the moment, and he didn't want to take a chance on lousing them up, and maybe losing his bedmate for the night.

Slocum wasn't stupid.

They were having to travel at a walk. Going any faster seemed to make the baby cry, and if there was one thing Slocum was sick of, it was that.

'Course, he figured that it likely wasn't the kid's fault. Only a few days old, already orphaned, and on starvation rations to boot. Hell, he should've been born in a nice, soft bed. He should have been spending his nights in a cradle, built by his daddy's own two hands, instead of on the hard desert floor, holed up in caves.

"They can't catch up to us, can they?" Lydia asked, out of the blue.

Slocum snorted. "Those Frame brothers? No way in hell!"

Billy Cree heard them before he saw them.

He rode quietly around a bend in a shallow canyon to spy the two misfits he'd been trailing, arguing and shouting to beat the band. One of them—the one pulling the travois—had his hat off and, with it, was slapping the holy shit out of the other man.

Billy whoaed up his horse and scowled. Now, what in the hell had he gotten himself into?

It crossed his mind that he might be doing the whole Southwest a big favor if he just skinned his gun and shot them, right here and now.

But then, they might have some interesting things to say about this fellow that the Kid's woman had gotten mixed up with.

Whoever he was, he'd sure done them some damage, all right. Not only was the one with the crutch still bleeding from time to time, but his friend was shot in the shoulder, too. At least he appeared to be since his shoulder was bandaged.

Billy urged his horse forward again.

But he drew his gun, just in case these boys were the nervous sort. You never could tell.

He rode within twenty feet of them before the fellow getting hit with the hat peeked up long enough to spot him.

He rode up another ten feet and stopped his mount before the fellow getting beat could get the other one's attention.

By the time the fellow doing the whomping stopped what he was doing and looked over at Billy, Billy was all relaxed, leaning forward in the saddle, his forearm on the saddle horn, and grinning.

"You boys are right entertainin'," he said, by way of hello. "You put on this show for all your company, or is this here just for me?"

The one with the crutch squinted at him and said, "Huh?"

The other slapped his hat back on his head and said, "Who the hell are you?"

Well, Billy thought with a smug little grin, *I guess we know who's in charge now, don't' we?*

"Billy Cree," Billy said right out, "and proud of it. You yokels got monikers?"

"We ain't yokels," said the one with the crutch. "We're from Texarkana."

Billy couldn't hold back a roll of his eyes, which only pinched the scab on his forehead and made him wince. "That right?" he said dryly.

"Yeah," said the other man. To his companion, he snarled, "And shut up, Ed, for Christ's sake."

Billy tipped his hat. "Howdy, Ed. You got a last name?"

Ed scrunched his mouth up and turned his head away like he wasn't going to talk, no matter what, but the other one said, "Frame. I'm Charlie. This here idiot's my brother."

"Pleased, boys," Billy said, smooth as butter. "Looked to me like you might be in a peck of trouble from the look of the trail back aways." He poked a thumb back over his shoulder.

"And you might be in some yourself, Mister Billy Cree, if'n you don't holster that smokewagon," said Charlie, bold as brass.

Now, Billy couldn't figure out how Charlie figured to get the drop on him, but he smiled good-naturedly and slid his gun home. He didn't replace the trigger strap, though.

"Better?" he asked.

"Some," replied Charlie.

"So," Billy said, "now that we're through with the amenities and pleasantries and stuff, who'd you run into back there that left you all shot to hell and on foot to boot?"

"A feller," piped up Ed. "He could'a done worse, though. Could'a killed us."

"Shut up, Ed," said Charlie and made like he was going to grab his hat again.

Ed ducked.

But Charlie didn't grab his hat. Instead, he said, "Big fella. Meaner than sin. Mayhap you heard of him?"

"Might have, if I knew his name," Billy replied. These boys were too stupid to live. He figured he just might shoot them after all, on general principle.

"Slocum," said Charlie, with some degree of pride. "*The* Slocum."

If Billy hadn't had a good hold on his saddle, he just might have fallen clean off his horse.

15

He recovered himself, though. He leaned farther forward, over his horse's neck, and said, "Aw, you're joshin' me, ain't you, boys?"

These two had survived a run-in with the famous Slocum? He could scarcely believe it!

Now, Billy Cree had been around. He'd never run into Slocum, but he'd heard plenty of things about him. And all over the West, not just here in the Arizona Territory. He'd listened to stories about Slocum stopping range wars single-handedly and Slocum taking down this man or another, Slocum's love for the ladies, and just tales about Slocum, the man.

Why, he'd sort of secretly hoped that one day he'd be as well-known—and feared—as Slocum!

One thing was sure: From the yarns he'd heard, Billy figured Slocum wasn't the type to allow the likes of these two bedbugs to live once they'd crossed him.

"What?" asked Charlie. He looked a mite irritated. "You callin' us liars?"

"No, sir, wouldn't do that." Billy scratched the back of his ear. "What did this Slocum feller look like?"

"Big," said Ed. He took advantage of the respite to sit

down on the desert floor and rest his leg. He seemed over-
ly interested in the tourniquet he had on it, and fiddled
with it constantly. "Big feller. Not fat-big, just tall and
real stronglike. Dark hair. Mean-lookin'."

"Funny eyes," Charlie added reluctantly. "Funny color,
I mean. Can't remember exactly. Might have been green."

"Scarred up?" asked Billy.

"Seen a few where his duds didn't cover 'em," Charlie
said. "Listen mister, you can just get the hell on your way
if'n you don't believe me. Run into him for your own
self. You'll see."

Well, it sure sounded like the Slocum that Billy'd been
hearing about all these years. Hot damn!

He asked, "He have anybody with him?"

Ed nodded. "A lady and a baby."

"Shut up, Ed," Charlie growled, and kicked at Ed's
hurt leg.

Ed yelped, but said no more.

Now, that was odd, Billy thought. Why the hell would
they care whether or not he knew who Slocum's traveling
companion was? And where in the devil did they pick up
a baby? Of course, the lady fit the legend of Slocum. It
figured that the whore would pick up with somebody like
him.

It didn't much matter right at the moment, he guessed.
He said, "That lady with Slocum. Her name Lydia? Lydia
West?"

Ed nodded his head in the affirmative, but kept his
mouth shut. Tears were still welling in his eyes from the
last kick administered by his brother.

"What's it to you, Mr. Billy Cree?" Charlie demanded.
"You got you some business with this woman?"

Billy gathered his reins and sat up straight. "Maybe."
His scalp was itching again where he'd sewn it together,
but he didn't take the time to scratch it. He flexed the
fingers on his gun hand.

"Ain't you gonna help us?" Ed asked at last from the ground. There was a little trickle of blood slowly working its way down his leg toward the ground, and his voice sounded pitiful.

" 'Fraid not, boys," Billy said. He pointed toward Ed's leg. "You know, you're gonna bleed to death if'n you don't cauterize that."

"Like you care," grumbled Ed, then looked up at Charlie. "What's cauterize?" he asked. "That like cuttin' a calf?"

Charlie ignored him, and Billy was well aware that his hand was hovering a little too near his gun. But Billy tipped his hat. He figured it was something that Slocum would do.

"Been nice, boys," he said, all smiles, "but I got to be about my business. You ain't got too much of a walk in front of you. You should make Cross Point by noon tomorrow."

"Hey!" Charlie angrily shouted. "Ain't you gonna take us along? Or at least leave us that spare pony?"

Billy just smiled. He reined his pinto horse away, although he kept his eyes on the one named Charlie. He didn't trust these boys much further than he could throw MacNulty's barn.

Charlie held his gaze, too, turning as Billy skirted them.

And then Billy did one of his tricks, one of the things he hoped he'd be famous for one day. He spun that pinto halfway around, and backed all the way down the little canyon, still leading the bay and keeping his eyes on the Frame brothers without cease. He backed that horse up almost a hundred yards in a straight line before he doffed his hat, spun the horse one hundred and eighty degrees, and took off at a gallop.

That ought to give those boys something to tell their kids, he thought. *They can tell 'em all about the time they were spared by the great Billy Cree, and about his fancy pony-work.*

He quickly picked up Slocum and Lydia's trail again, and once he was around a bend in the trail and out of the Frame brothers' sight, he slowed to a jog.

Well, he had some trouble getting the bay on the end of his lead rope to slow down, too, but he did it. He was glad he was out of the Frame brothers' sight, though.

And Slocum! Of all the rotten luck! He would have rather met up with Slocum in a saloon or someplace. Would have rather met him friendly than like this.

Was it worth taking a chance on getting his head blown off just to extract a little revenge on the bitch? He wasn't quite so sure, now. But then, he was the man who had hunted the Show Low Kid for a couple of years, and all for his half of about seven measly grand, which the Kid had long since spent.

And maybe taking down Slocum would be a good thing. It would sure seal his reputation.

That was, if he *could* take Slocum down.

From all the stories he'd listened to and the reverence and admiration and downright awe with which they had been told to him, this Slocum must have some kind of angel sitting on his shoulder. Either that, or he was just that much better than everybody else.

"Well, I ain't no slouch my own damn self," Billy muttered, and almost believed his own words. Still . . .

His gaze riveted to the track, he made his way along the trail. Billy Cree had a whole lot of hard thinking to do.

Lydia fed the baby the last of the milk before she ate her own lunch. It wasn't much. Just hardtack and coffee, but blessed with a couple of tiny desert quail that Slocum had shot.

They had stopped to take the noontime break at the

base of a hill, near a little clump of palo verde trees, bright
yellow with heavy spring bloom. Slocum had told her that
there was water here, underground, which didn't come to
the surface until farther on, just outside Cross Point.

Rivers that ran underground, scorpions slipping into
the shoes under her bed at night, miles of desert with no
civilization in sight: to all these things and more she had
grown accustomed since she came to Arizona.

It was different back home. Cedar Rapids, Iowa, that's
where she was from. It was green there. Green and rolling,
with rich soil. You could smell it, that black, black, Iowa
dirt. You could smell the richness of it, and the promise
of it.

It occurred to her that maybe she should go back home.
Maybe not to Cedar Rapids, where a scandal had run her
out of town and driven her west in the first place. But
some other town in Iowa. Or to be safe, Illinois. She had
a different name now, didn't she?

"How's your quail? Sorry there isn't more."

Lydia looked up and smiled. How fortunate, how very
fortunate she was to have been found by Slocum and
gifted with this baby. She knew little about children, but
she found herself growing fonder and fonder of the red-
headed tyke.

And as for Slocum?

She knew he wouldn't stay. He wasn't the type, and
the good Lord was aware that she'd known all too many
of them. No, he wouldn't stay. But he'd given her succor
and tenderness and release—and hope—at a time when
she'd needed it most.

She'd remember him in her prayers for the rest of her
days.

And she'd thank him again, too, once they got to town.

The smile escaped her lips, and she felt herself blush
a little. She said, "It's fine. Just wonderful! What do you
think? Maybe a couple more hours?"

Slocum nodded. He sat next to her, picking the roasted quail off the bones with his fingers. "Considerin' that we have to travel so slow, I figure we're makin' pretty decent time."

He tipped his torso to one side, and it took her a half second to realize he was trying to see the baby, which she'd wrapped in a blanket. "Tyler asleep?" he asked.

"For the moment," she said. "Slocum?"

"Yes'm?"

"I've been thinking," she started, choosing her words carefully. "About what I want to do after we get to Cross Point, that is."

He arched a brow and waited.

"Do you think," she said hesitantly, "I mean, if he doesn't have any other relatives or anything, that they'd give Tyler to me? To raise?"

He looked a little surprised at the question. He said, "I don't know, Lydia. 'Course, I don't see why not." He shrugged those big shoulders. "Hell, he's likely got plenty of money to support the both of you for a long spell."

"Oh," she said, blinking. "I hadn't thought of that. The mine, I mean. I was thinking about maybe taking him back east."

"It's a thought," Slocum said, and after tossing the last of the quail bones over his shoulder, licked his greasy fingers clean, muttering, "Hell, that wasn't much more than an appetizer."

Lydia chuckled. "You'll get the meal tonight," she whispered. "And dessert."

He leaned over and cupped her face in his hand. "You mean what I think you mean, honey?" he said, grinning a little wickedly.

"Only if you have a very dirty mind, Mr. Slocum," she said, the corners of her mouth crooking up.

He looked around, leaned a little closer, and asked, "Why are we whispering?"

"Little nippers have big ears," she said softly, and tipped her head toward the sleeping baby.

Slocum's smile turned into a full-fledged grin. "The kid's gotta learn sometime," he said, and kissed her.

"Goddamn it, Ed, get up!" Charlie shouted. They had walked almost another mile since meeting up with Billy Cree, and Charlie was still madder than a hornet. "And stop bleedin'!" he added.

"It ain't my fault if I'm still leakin'!" Ed shouted back. He was down on the ground again, and holding his leg, and he was mad at his brother, too. "It hurts, Charlie! Can't we stop for a while? Ain't no way in hell we're gonna catch 'em, even if we was to run dead-out. I swan, if we don't stop and have us a break pretty damn soon, I'm gonna up and die on you. Then you'll be sorry!"

Charlie started to make a grab for his hat and Ed ducked his head, but then Charlie seemed to think better of it.

"Oh, hellfire," he said, and slumped to the ground, too.

He wiped his sleeve over his brow, eyed his brother, and said, "You're right, Ed. You couldn't catch up with 'em, even if you was to run. Your pin is pretty damned bad, I'll admit that. So here's the deal. I'm gonna have me a little break here with you, and then I'm gonna go on by my lonesome."

Ed opened his mouth as if to complain, but Charlie held up a hand. He held it close enough to his hat that Ed closed his yap.

"I'm gonna come back for you," Charlie went on, in a way that Ed didn't think was entirely unbelievable, "don't you worry. And I'm leavin' you half the water and grub. Not that there's much. But by God, I ain't gonna let a whole gold mine slip away, not when I'm so close to grabbin' it!"

But Ed was still worried. What if Charlie went and got

himself killed up there? His brow furrowed. "Don't leave me, Charlie," he said, a plea in his voice. "Let it go this time."

"Got to," Charlie replied.

Now, Ed figured that Charlie's arm must be hurting him terrible, but it was worse for having to haul that travois. Charlie could make better time if he was only carrying supplies for one person. And Charlie's leg wasn't banged up like Ed's was. Charlie could step up the pace if he wasn't having to go so slow for Ed.

Ed wasn't as stupid as Charlie thought.

Charlie was saying, "You can see that I got to, can't you, Ed? I gotta do it for us."

Ed didn't say anything. He knew Charlie well enough to know that Charlie wanted that gold mine, period. It didn't matter that Ed was sort of in on it, too. It was the money, or the promise of money, that had Charlie's innards in an uproar.

Oh, if Ed was still alive when Charlie rode back for him—and he probably would be, because Ed was one pretty lucky sonofabitch, even if he did say so himself— then Charlie would share and share alike. Blood was blood, after all.

But the money was the thing that was keeping Charlie's nose to the track.

"Can't you see, Ed?" Charlie urged.

Ed took a deep breath, then whistled it out through his teeth. He didn't say so, but he'd agree to just about anything to get off his feet for another fifteen minutes or so.

Slowly, he nodded his head.

"I reckon," he said at last. "I reckon I can see how you got to go on. You're gonna go on without me, anyhow, so I might's well give it my blessin'." Then he looked up. "But Charlie, I still don't see how you're gonna catch up with them. They're probably near to town by now!"

Charlie began to take his things off the travois and put

them in a little pile. "That ain't my first whatchacall . . . objective, Ed."

"What is, then?"

"Gonna catch up to that goddamn Billy Cree, that no-account, gun-happy little bastard," Charlie spat. "He didn't think I ever heard of him, but I have, all right. Damn little pipsqueak. He thinks he's so high and mighty on account of he's held up a few stages and one lousy bank!"

That was it, then, Ed thought, or at least a big part of it. Ed wondered just how long it would take him to walk to town. Charlie was bound and determined to take on both Slocum and this Cree fellow, whoever the hell he was. Ed had sure never heard of him.

'Course, he'd never heard of Slocum either. Maybe Charlie was right. He needed to pay more attention to what folks said.

But to lose a gold mine and a brother—and maybe his own leg—all in two days? Why, it was insulting, that was what! Kind of sad-making, too.

Charlie, who was still caught up in thoughts of vengeance and riches and hadn't seen the trace of insight flicker over Ed's features, snorted. "Well, he ain't seen the last of Charlie Frame, no sir! He's up there somewhere, and he's got him a horse, that's a horse I want. I want both of 'em! The goddamn gall of him, to ride through here with that spare mount and not even offer to let one of us ride it!"

Ed was pretty sure which one of them Charlie meant, but didn't say anything.

"I'm gonna get me that sonofabitch Slocum next," Charlie went on, "and then I'm gonna get that damn baby and the mine!"

Charlie stood, scooped up his possessions, and straightened his hat. "I'll be back for you, Ed," he said and set off, at a considerably more rapid pace, toward the east.

Ed sat there, watching him retreat into the distance. "Good luck, there, Charlie," he muttered, and absently twisted the stick in his tourniquet again.

16

Slocum helped Lydia up from the ground, then brushed the dust from his clothes. He was disappointed that she'd called a halt to the proceedings—well, disappointed wasn't exactly the word for it. Blue balls was closer. But he had to agree that it was foolish to stop here, when they were so close to town, and could have things so much better.

And softer.

And safer.

"Sorry," Lydia said again as she batted at her skirts. The dust rose in little clouds.

"No, you're right, honey. Don't worry about it no more." He went to the horses and began to tighten their girths.

Behind him, she said, "Slocum?"

"I told you, baby, I'm all right," he lied. "We'll be in town in a couple of hours, and then—"

"Slocum!"

He turned to see a rider bearing down on them. It wasn't one of the Frame boys, that was for sure. This man was riding all out, low over his horse's neck as only a shorter man could.

131

And in his hand, something flashed silver in the sun.

Without ceremony, Slocum shoved Lydia to the ground with a shout of, "Get to cover!"

He didn't see where she got to, because he dropped and rolled the other way just as a slug hit the dirt right in the spot where he'd been standing.

It wouldn't have killed him, but it wouldn't have done his foot a whole lot of good, either.

His rifle was in his boot on Tubac, who, along with the other horses, had skittered to one side at the sound of the shot.

Slocum was stuck with just his handgun. It would have to do. He already had it free of its holster and was steadying his hand, preparing to squeeze off a shot at the charging gunman.

But at the split second that he fired, the man in the distance wheeled his horse to one side and brought him to a sliding stop. He bounded from the horse's back before he had stopped all the way, and dove behind a cluster of rocks.

"Shit," Slocum muttered.

Quickly, he looked over to see where Lydia and the baby had got to. He saw a little of the fabric of her skirt peeking from behind a low rock. She was safe, and she had the baby with her. At least, Tyler and the blanket seemed to have vanished from their former position on the ground.

Well, she had a lot better cover than he did, damn it. There wasn't anything this way but weeds and a couple of stunted bushes, by which he was barely concealed. Again, he swore.

He wished he had that rifle, if only to toss it to Lydia. She'd already proven that she knew how to lay down a good covering fire. She was a damn good shot, too.

Good, hell! She'd shot Charlie from about fifty yards out!

"Slocum?" she said quietly, from behind her rock. "Slocum, are you all right?"

And just then, he had a thought. A stroke of pure genius, more like. Whoever was out there must have passed the Frame brothers and who the hell knew what had passed between them? But it was a pretty sure bet that the gunman was either after Slocum—it could have been for a hundred different things, including just wanting to hone his own reputation by adding Slocum to his list of kills—or else he was after the baby, and the baby's deed to that mine.

In any case, it was a sure thing that the gunman knew that Slocum was right here.

And maybe it might be better if the gunman thought Slocum was dead.

"I'm fine," he shouted back at Lydia, and immediately covered his head with his hands.

It was just in time, too, because a barrage of shots came right at him, kicking up dirt and weeds. One slug snaked across his shoulder, burning like hell. For once, he did what he felt like doing. He hollered good and loud.

"Slocum!" shouted Lydia.

"Stay put," he hissed.

"Slocum, are you hurt?"

Damn the woman, anyway. Why couldn't she just let a fellow pretend to be dead?

"I'm fine," he hissed, just loud enough for her to hear, and in spite of the blood trickling down his arm and back. "Just start wailin' over me, all right?"

"But I—" she began, and then said, "Oh!"

Suddenly, she began to keen. "Oh, Slocum! You've shot Slocum, you son of a skunk! What will I do now? Slocum, please! Slocum, move! Don't be dead!"

Hell, a man at three times this yahoo's distance could have heard her plain. What lungs!

He believed he saw a little rustle in the grass next to that clump of rock.

Lydia whispered, "That's Billy Cree's horse out there. I don't know who's got it or why."

"Let's worry about it later, all right?" Slocum muttered.

Out across the canyon, a man slowly and warily stood up, back behind the rocks.

Lydia's head popped up over the rocks, and absolute fury filled her face. She cried, at the top of her lungs, "Billy Cree, you murdering, raping sonofabitch! Why aren't you dead?"

Slocum mouthed a curse word that he wouldn't have repeated loud enough for Lydia to hear. This was just wonderful, all right. Lydia said that she'd killed Billy Cree!

Just how many more dead men were there out there, gunning for them?

But he didn't have long to be annoyed. Lydia knew what she was doing, after all. She kept on shouting at Billy, harassing him, and he confidently began to walk forward.

"You shut up, you slab-sided bitch!" Billy shouted. "You know damn well what I'm gonna do when I get my hands on you."

"Ha!" Lydia called back. "*If* you do, you mean."

"When!" Billy shouted. "I'm gonna do you again like I done you at the Kid's, and when I'm tired of you, gonna take my gun and put it to your head and send you home to Jesus. Or hell."

"I'll rip your dinky little pecker off before I'll let you poke me again with it!"

Despite himself, Slocum blinked at that one. In fact, he lost his concentration entirely.

"Like hell you will, you little whore!" Billy shouted again, and Slocum snapped back to business.

Now, he could have shot Billy right there, probably killed him or at least wounded him, but he didn't want to kill him. No, Slocum wanted to haul Billy Cree into town with his tail between his legs. It would serve the little sonofabitch right.

In the words of somebody-or-other, killing was too good for this pipsqueak.

So he let Billy and Lydia yell more nasty things at each other, let Lydia coax Billy into a false sense of security as to Slocum's status, until he was within thirty feet of that rock.

He squeezed the trigger.

Billy's hat went flying and he got off a shot in response, but it went wild. A surprised look frozen on his face, he fell to his knees, then forward, splat out on the ground.

Lydia popped up—all the way to her feet, this time.

"Did you get him?" she demanded. "Is he dead?"

"Hope not," Slocum said, and got to his feet. "And get the hell down, Lydia, till I see if he's within reach of his gun."

She didn't budge. She pointed. "It went way over there."

He saw it. He nodded. He turned, yanked the rope off Tubac's saddle and his rifle from the boot and proceeded to walk out to Billy.

He was only halfway there when Lydia cried, "You're hurt!"

"Told you I was," he said over his shoulder. But he said it with a grin. Billy looked to be all the way out of it, but still breathing. His torso softly rose and fell with each breath.

Slocum kept the nose of his rifle pointed at him, anyway.

"And stay there, damn it," he called as he came to a stop over Billy's body. He heard weeds rustle as Lydia returned to her roost, and without thinking, grinned again.

Billy's skull was creased right along the back, about a half inch down from where Slocum had been aiming. It was a pretty fair shot with a Colt, he thought, especially for a twice-shot man trying to lie flat in the weeds.

Still, he could have done it better.

But it wasn't like he could do it over again, so he merely stuck the rifle's barrel under Billy and levered him over onto his back.

Out cold.

"That's a good little gunslinger," Slocum muttered, and began to tie him up.

17

Charlie Frame trudged on at a dull jog.

His legs, unaccustomed to traveling afoot, were about to give out and his shoulder was killing him. He had dropped, in fact, everything he carried but his food and water. The only thing keeping him going now was the sheer hatred that a certain kind of man develops when he imagines he's been humiliated beyond comprehension.

And that's exactly what Charlie figured had happened to him.

The baby, and the mine, had ceased to be a glittering possibility. They had become his by rights, snatched from him when his back was turned. That it wasn't his baby, or his mine—or that his back hadn't been turned at all—no longer occurred to him.

Slocum deserved to die for taking that kid away, and Billy Cree deserved no less a death for thinking he was better than Charlie Frame.

Goddamn it, anyway! Better? No man was better than Charlie Frame!

The facts of the matter didn't bother Charlie too much. They never had. He was too bent on himself and what he could get out of any particular situation. Even the thought of Ed, far behind by now, hurt, alone, and abandoned, was far from his mind.

What was a lousy brother compared to a fortune and sweet revenge?

Charlie, despite the heat, despite his weary legs and his throbbing shoulder, smiled.

And then he stopped, stock-still.

Gunshots echoed through the air. He couldn't tell where it came from by the sounds of it. There were too many twists and turns in here, and the sounds bounced too many ways. But he knew the sounds could only have come from one direction. Ahead, no matter how many twists and turns there were to it.

His legs filled with a new charge of energy, he broke into a dead run, the water bag slapping, unfelt, at his back.

And strangely enough, he was praying, praying that Billy Creed had polished off that goddamn Slocum for good. Then there'd be only one for him to settle things with.

'Course, there'd only be one, any way a fellow looked at it, wouldn't there?

Then they really began tearing it up. Six shots, real fast!

Charlie moved as fast as his tired legs would carry him, which was with surprising speed. His breath came in huge gulps and pants, and he felt that his heart would pound out of his chest and his lungs would burst, but still he ran and ran and ran.

And then, much closer now, he heard a single shot.

He nearly tripped and fell smack on his face, he stopped so fast.

It had sounded like the last of a gunfight to him. Somebody had won, he'd put his money on that. But which one?

"You ain't gonna find out if you stand here all day," he muttered between pants. Steeling himself, forgetting even to grab himself a quick gulp of water, he took off at a long-legged lope.

A few minutes later, utterly breathless, Charlie stopped and bent over, hands on his knees, gasping for air. And while he was in that position, nose to knees, he heard something.

A horse?

Yes, indeed! It wasn't a mirage or a trick of the mind. There was a real-life bay pony standing maybe a hundred yards off. Saddled and bridled, too!

It took him a second to realize it was the spare that Billy Cree had been leading.

"Sonofabitch!" Charlie wheezed, then tried to laugh and coughed instead. "Son of a goddamn bitch!"

He set off toward it.

Except the damned horse didn't want to be caught. Once he got within three feet of snagging a rein, the blasted thing suddenly wheeled and trotted away.

But Charlie was bent on going the rest of the way astride. He didn't give a thought to taking the horse back and picking up Ed. No, his intention, and his only thought, was to get a grip on that goddamn bangtail and go barreling after Billy Cree or Slocum, whichever one had come out on top, and to lay his hands on the baby and its mine.

"Nice horse," he whispered as he crept up on it again. "Good horse. Once I get my hands on you," he soothed, "I'm gonna have you turned into glue."

Again, the horse skittered away, then stopped about fifty yards away.

"Goddamn it!" Charlie breathed, and started toward it all over again.

Slocum sat still, albeit unwillingly, while Lydia bandaged his shoulder.

"Ain't necessary," he said for at least the tenth time. "It's just a scratch."

"I'll be the judge of what is and isn't a scratch, Slocum," Lydia said crossly, although he could tell by her tone that she was joshing. "My Lord, is your hobby getting yourself banged up? I've never seen so many scars in my life on one person. Not even on ten people, combined!"

He chuckled, low. "Just unlucky, that's all."

"No," she said, "pretty gosh-darned lucky, if I'm any judge. At least half of these wounds would have killed another man."

He cast his eye toward the horses, where Billy Cree lay, unconscious and trussed like a Christmas goose. Still no movement.

"I been told that before," he replied. "Suppose folks are right. I'm beginnin' to feel like one great big hunk of scar tissue, though."

Lydia stood up and dusted her hands. "You can put your shirt back on, now," she said, shaking her pretty head. "You are one tough bird, Slocum."

"Been told that, too," he said with a smile. "Like usual, folks are probably right." He shrugged his sleeve back on, although carefully. That scratch still stung like Hades. " 'Cept they usually put an 'old' in there, before the bird part."

Lydia, grinning, snorted softly. "We ready to go now?"

"Soon's I get Billy there loaded up on a horse," he said, and swatted at a bee. He missed.

She looked disappointed. "Why load him up? I thought we could just drag him."

"By God, Lydia, if I didn't know better, I'd think you were bloodthirsty."

She cocked her head. "You know what they say about a woman scorned, Slocum? Well, that's nothing compared

Checkout Receipt

Library name: N

Current time: 07/31/2014,15:33
Title: Slocum and the Orphan
Express
Call number: LOGAN
Item ID: 33206005636455
Date due: 8/14/2014,23:59

Total checkouts for session: 1
Total checkouts: 1

Renew by phone at
577-3977
or online at
www.sanleandrolibrary.org

to a woman wronged. Hell would be a paradise compared to what I'd like to do to that scum you've got trussed up over there."

"Remind me never to wrong you, Lydia," he said, one eyebrow raised. "Even in the tiniest way. Hate to get on your bad side."

And then he remembered, belatedly, exactly what Billy Cree had done to get on Lydia's bad side, and he said, "Sorry, honey. I didn't mean that like it sounded. I wouldn't blame you if you were to take my gun and shoot the bastard through the head, instead of just grazin' it, like I did."

She merely sighed and said, "Let's get on with it, Slocum. The sooner we get his backside in a jail cell, the better."

Slocum heaved Billy up and slung him across his pinto's saddle with some difficulty. Billy was smallish and fairly lightweight, but his body pressed on Slocum's twice-wounded shoulder.

He tied Billy's bound hands to one stirrup and then passed the rope under the horse's belly, through the other stirrup, and around his bound boots. And then, for added security, he ran the rope through Billy's belt at the side, and tied it snugly to the saddle horn with a breakaway knot.

"That ought to hold you, you little bastard," he muttered, and gave Billy's thigh a sharp pop with his hand.

The baby had started crying again, and Lydia was pacing up and down, singing softly to him to no avail.

"What's that matter with him?" he asked.

"Good question," Lydia replied. "He doesn't need changing. I checked. And he was fed not that long ago. I think it's just getting to him, Slocum. I know it's gotten to me, being out here for so long." She lowered her face and nuzzled the crying Tyler. "Poor baby, poor tyke," she said softly.

"Well, let's give him what he wants," Slocum said, and led one of the spare horses over to her. "I'll be mighty glad to get into a town, too."

He held out his arms for the squalling baby so that Lydia could mount. He watched her skirts swishing over her shapely backside as she swung a leg over the horse. "Mighty glad," he repeated.

"When's the last time you were in Cross Point?" she asked as she took the baby from him.

Slocum shrugged. "I don't know. Three, maybe four years ago. Why?"

"I think you'll find it changed," she said, gathering the reins in her free hand. "I was last there about seven or eight months ago. Their silver's petering out. It was still a fair-sized town, but only about half as big as it used to be."

"Makes sense," Slocum said. He straightened out the spare horse's lead rope and Billy's horse's lead, then swung a leg over Tubac. "They got the river comin' up for about a mile's worth down there, but the soil's bad for farming. Dirt doesn't grow enough grass for ranching, either. Without the silver for a lure, can't see as how many folks would want to live there."

He clucked to Tubac and the horse moved out, the others bringing up the rear. Lydia jogged up alongside him, then slowed to a walk to keep pace. Over the baby's cries, she said, "I hope you're right. I mean, you probably are. When I was there last, folks had enough truck gardens growing along the riverbanks to feed them for a little while. Just hope the sheriff's still hanging around."

Slocum reached across the space between them and briefly gripped her forearm. In this heated world of dry, hard things, it felt like cool silk.

"Don't fret, honeylamb," he said, loud enough to be heard over the crying baby. "If there ain't any sheriff, I'll take Billy Cree on to someplace where there is one. He's gonna get what's comin' to him. You can count on that."

He meant it, too.

Exhausted and wheezing, Charlie Frame finally cornered the bay, and gave it a hit upside the head, once he had the reins firmly in his grip.

The horse half-reared, but Charlie hung on, then tightened the girth and climbed up into the saddle. He gave that pony a kick and took off at a gallop.

He supposed he knew why Billy had let that horse loose. He was close to town. He wouldn't need two, and leading the bay would have slowed him down. 'Course, Charlie couldn't figure why he'd left the saddle and bridle on it. Well, who was he to judge? The fact was that Billy had abandoned the horse, and it was now his. Possession was nine-tenths of the law, wasn't it?

He slowed down and stopped at the top of the shallow rise from which Billy Cree had ridden down on Slocum and Lydia, his guns blazing.

Charlie's guns weren't blazing though, and—for the moment, anyway—he wasn't trying to catch Slocum and Lydia. Screwing up his face, he watched as the back ends of their horses plodded off into the distance.

He had no doubt about who had won the gun battle that he'd heard. It was Slocum. You couldn't mistake the rump of that Appaloosa horse of his. And there was a man-sized bundle tied over the saddle of Billy Cree's pinto.

The thin sound of a far-off baby crying carried on the wind.

"Goddamn sonofabitch!" Charlie huffed, and choked

on his words. He hadn't started out in the best of shape, and the gallop had left him breathless.

After a fit of coughing, during which he was sure he'd cough up his spleen any second, he refrained from further words until he'd taken a long drink of water.

And even then, he didn't speak.

Just you wait, Slocum, he thought angrily. *Just you wait.*

He sat there until he could no longer see Slocum and Lydia, which wasn't much of a trick. They had turned left, into another warren of hill and valley and canyon. But he sat until he was breathing even again. And then he coaxed the horse beneath him into a walk.

He'd catch them, all right, he thought as he rode slowly along. He'd catch up to them in town, and wouldn't they be surprised to see him! Especially when he announced to the sheriff that the man who'd ridden in with that baby was the one-and-only Slocum, a dog if ever there was one.

Why, he'd say that he was the baby's rightful uncle! He'd say that Slocum and Lydia had kidnapped it while he was on a mission of mercy to save it, and that they wouldn't turn loose of it for beans. Plus which, they'd shot up him and his poor brother, who was still up in the hills.

For the first time in a good long while, Charlie smiled. Why, if this one worked out, he might just switch from being a man of action to being a man of many lies! 'Course, he was already that, but it didn't stop him from daydreaming.

And they weren't that far ahead. They were going slow. He'd likely make town right after they did. His water bag was lighter, now, too. That would help.

Still plodding, he rummaged in his things for his food

sack, pulled out the last of the corn dodgers he'd hidden from his brother and the tail end of his jerky, and tossed their wrappers to the desert floor behind him.

Chewing, he marched on.

18

Ed Frame had found a surprising new well of energy about a half an hour after his brother, Charlie, left. He wasn't certain where it had come from, although if he'd thought about it long and hard, he might have decided that its roots were in desperation.

He hadn't made very good time. Not nearly so good as Charlie was likely to be able to make. But he had limped and dragged himself a good mile. Now, he sat in the feeble shade of the low cliff face, toying with his tourniquet and drinking warm water from one of the canteens.

It was just like Charlie to take the water bag and leave him with two lousy canteens, wasn't it?

Well, Charlie was Charlie. Ed guessed he couldn't help it, just the same as he couldn't help killing that Mr. Tyler and going after the baby. Just like he couldn't help but kill Sam Jeffords over a card game last year, and that farmer, whatshisname, the year before that.

Ed had sort of liked that farmer. His wife had cooked them a good meal, too. Didn't seem quite fair when Charlie plugged him in the back just to get his old roan riding horse.

But Ed hadn't said anything.

He never said much of anything, really.

Charlie complained about not being as famous as Billy Cree, and he was sort of right. Ed thought that with all the killings that Charlie had done, Charlie really ought to be celebrated. 'Course, Charlie cut his own legs out from under himself, making his murders all secret-like. It seemed to Ed that Charlie maybe should tell somebody, or else gun them down in front of witnesses if he wanted credit for killing people.

But then, Ed thought, shrugging, *what the hell do I know?*

At least, that was what Charlie was always telling him.

Rested, he capped his canteen and slowly worked his way up to his feet and got his crutch under his arm. His leg was bleeding a lot less, now that he was going at his own pace instead of trying to keep up with Charlie.

He thought he just might fool everybody, Charlie included, and live.

Slowly, he limped his way along the trail.

It didn't look right. Not right at all.

Slocum moved his spyglass over a little to the right, then to the left, but there still were no signs of life to be seen in Cross Point. Just tumbleweeds in the streets, busted signs barely clinging to their posts, no people, no livestock.

"Bad news," he said, lowering the spyglass.

"What?" Lydia asked.

"I don't think anybody's home," he said grimly, and moved Tubac into a walk. "And you shut up," he said to Billy Cree, who had regained consciousness about an hour out of town, but remained tied, facedown, across his saddle.

"Didn't say nothin', you goddamn sonofa—"

Slocum slapped him across the back with the ends of

his reins, and Billy yelped, "Ouch!" instead of finishing his sentence.

"There's a lady present, boy," Slocum lectured, "so just mind your tongue."

"Lady, my shiny pink ass," Billy quipped.

Slocum answered him with another cut of the reins, to which Billy gave the usual response.

"Ouch!"

"Be nice, or when we get into town, I'll turn her loose and look the other way," Slocum said. "You gettin' my point?"

Silence was all that issued from Billy, although he might have muttered something into the saddle leather. Slocum didn't know, and frankly, he didn't care.

But Lydia piped up, "Love to, Slocum. You'll tie him up so that he can't move—other than to scream, I mean— no matter what I do to him?"

He looked over at her. She was grinning, but there seemed to be a thread of seriousness running through her threat. He couldn't say he blamed her much.

Slocum smiled back. "Promise."

"I hope there's still a jail cell with a working lock on it," she said.

Slocum grunted. He'd been thinking about that, as well.

"But at least we'll have the hotel all to ourselves," Lydia went on hopefully. "I just pray that the mercantile isn't completely cleaned out." She lifted her gaze upward. "Just a few cans of milk, Lord, that's all I ask for."

"There might be a few people left down there," Slocum said, trying his best to sound optimistic. He wasn't counting on any milk for miles around, which didn't bode too well for little Tyler. "Towns usually take longer than this to die out all the way."

He didn't add that at the very end, they were usually

inhabited by the dregs of society. That was all he and
Lydia needed.

They neared the town and rode past a few deserted
houses. Their little yards were weedy, their truck gardens
had gone to pot, and abandoned tools rusted in their yards.
Many had broken windows. "Looks like somebody's had
their fun here already," he said.

Lydia didn't answer.

They crossed the wooden bridge that still stood across
the barely trickling river, and entered the town. Buildings
stood, their paint already peeling and their whitewash already cracking. The desert was hard on anything man-
made.

Dodging tumbleweeds, they rode down the center of
the main street, finding more shattered glass, more shut-
ters banging softly in the breeze, but no signs of life. Not
even a dog.

"There's the mercantile," Lydia piped up, and pointed.

Slocum reined Tubac toward it.

"You might's well turn me free and let me have my
way with her," Billy offered. "Ain't another town for
miles and miles."

"Shut up," Slocum snapped.

"Can I just shoot him, Slocum?" Lydia asked as Slocum reined in next to the hitching rail.

"Not now," he said, dismounting. He tossed Tubac's
reins over the rail, then walked around to help her with
the baby. "Maybe later."

"Looking forward to it," she said. She dismounted,
then took the baby from Slocum. She walked around
Billy's horse and slugged Billy, just as hard as she could,
in the ear.

"Hey!" shouted Billy. Tears came to his eyes.

"You sorry bastard," Lydia said. "As soon as I feed
this poor child, you're getting gelded."

"Listen, bitch, I—"

"Didn't I tell you to shut the hell up?" Slocum asked, and took a few steps toward Billy, who quieted and turned his head away. "C'mon, Lydia," he said, taking her arm. "Stop teasin' the prisoner."

Slocum didn't think things were looking too awful good. He found himself repeating Lydia's prayer that there'd be canned milk in the store.

They left Billy tied over his saddle and mounted the steps to the boardwalk, and Slocum had just put a hand to the mercantile's front door when a gravelly voice called out.

"Hey there! Stop, looters!" This last command was accompanied by the sound of a shotgun's double cock.

Slocum turned around to see a bandy-legged old coot standing about twenty yards away in the center of the street they had just ridden up. Although he looked more like a prospector—and one who hadn't had much luck as of late—there was a sheriff's badge pinned to his ragged shirt.

Slocum raised his arms. "We're not looters, Sheriff. And we brought you a prisoner."

The old man cocked his head and squinted toward Billy Cree. "He a real wild one?"

"Wild as they come," Slocum replied.

The sheriff walked a few steps closer, then stopped again. "You got a name?"

"I'm Slocum," Slocum said. "This lady's Mrs. Lydia West."

The sheriff took a few steps closer. "Put your hands down, young feller. You're makin' me nervous."

Slocum eased his arms down. He noticed the sheriff didn't lower his shotgun, though.

"And this young feller strapped acrost his pony?"

Slocum said, "This is your prisoner, Sheriff. One young hot-blood by the name of Billy Cree. He murdered Mrs. West's husband. Among other things."

Billy snorted into his saddle leather. He craned his head up and around and got a view of the sheriff. "Doubt this hole's got a cell strong enough to hold the likes of me, Sheriff," he said, his voice cocky and full of himself.

"Billy Cree," the sheriff mused. "Billy Cree. Yup, it seems to me like I've heard of him. 'Course, seems like I heard of you, too, Slocum."

The way he said it made Slocum's mouth crook up into a smile. "You want me to put my hands back up?"

The sheriff screwed up his face. "Nope. Heard more good than bad. That is, if you're the same one. You have a hand in that Bent's Arroyo business last year?"

"That I did," replied Slocum, suddenly wondering if the old man was going to shoot him or slap him on the back.

As it turned out, the sheriff did neither. Walking the rest of the way up to them, he said, "Well, now, I reckon you know my friend Cosmo Kulick." He waited expectantly.

"That I do," said Slocum, feeling a little like a kid who's been given a surprise test by his teacher. And he had no doubts that any man holding a Greener on him was in charge, all right.

"Cosmo's about five-foot-nothin'," he continued, "and slab-sided as a steer after a yearlong drought. Got him a black mustache the size of Tennessee, and he's one of the funniest bastards ever to come down from Canuck country."

Simultaneously, the sheriff broke out in a toothless grin and dropped the nose of his shotgun. "That's old Cosmo, all right. I heared you saved his life up there, so you're okay with me, Slocum." He offered a grimy hand. "My name's O'Keefe. Dusty O'Keefe. Sheriff, mayor, judge, chief bottle washer, and total population of Cross Point, Arizona Territory. At least, this week. Say! What's that you got there, ma'am? A baby?"

"We wondered if you'd have any milk," Lydia said, nodding. "He's in dire need."

Sheriff O'Keefe took off his floppy hat and bent his balding head in a semblance of a bow. "Mrs. West, is it? If we got any, it's in the mercantile, all right. Francis Clarke didn't take all his inventory to the grave with him."

Lydia looked shocked. "Mr. Clarke is dead? But he was a young man!"

"Oh, Francis were young, all right. Couldn't have been more'n thirty-five," O'Keefe said, nodding his head. He paused to slap his hat back in place. "That didn't mean nothin' to the wild bunch that rode through here about five months back. Francis got shot over a can of beans. Can you believe it? A dang can of plain lima beans! Didn't even have no meat in 'em!"

"Terrible," said Lydia.

"Dang right, it's terrible," O'Keefe said as he mounted the steps, then opened the mercantile's front door for her. "I owed Francis sixty cents, and didn't have a chance to get square with him. Ma'am?" he said as he ushered her in. "Take whatever you feel like you can use, and welcome to it. Francis would have wanted it that-a-way."

And then he turned to Slocum. "I'll be hanged. Slocum, right here in my town." He shook his head. "It surely is a small world, like my wife, Letty, used to say. A real small world. Now, what you say we take this here junior-grade killer on up to the jail?"

"Be glad to," Slocum said, and pulled the breakaway knot on the rope. Momentarily, Billy slid to the ground like a sack of beans, head first, and landed with a soft thump.

"Hey!" Billy yelped.

No one paid him any attention.

"And then," Slocum added, "I got a real interesting story to tell you."

O'Keefe lifted Billy from the ground with surprising

strength, Slocum thought, especially for a man as old and skinny as he was.

O'Keefe took Billy's arm in one bony hand and hefted his Greener in the other. "I'm lookin' forward to that, Slocum. Yessir, lookin' forward to it."

19

Lydia's eyes traveled over the dusty shelves until her gaze settled on tinned milk—a whole row of it! Sighing happily, she muttered, "Tyler, we just hit the treasure trove!"

The baby gurgled at her in response.

He was so good-natured. If she'd been him, she'd likely have been screaming her head off the whole way. Well, he almost had. Poor little thing.

She lay the child on the counter, after dusting it first with her sleeve—Sheriff O'Keefe might have been living off Francis Clarke's goods, but he certainly wasn't much of a housekeeper. Or a gourmet, either. The only shelves that showed signs of recent pillage contained the last few parcels of beans, canned and dried, and tinned meat.

O'Keefe seemed to favor potted pork.

After putting the baby down, she picked up a can of milk, then searched the store for something to open it with. Finding a can punch behind the counter, she opened the milk, then took a new bottle down from the shelves. It was bigger than Tyler's old one, and one more in proportion with his growing appetite.

Which was about to be fed.

She poured a little milk into the bottle, then went outside and poured an equal amount of water into it, shaking it as she went back inside.

She picked up the baby and sat down in Francis Clarke's old rocking chair. "Sorry it's still not warmed, Tyler," she said as the baby greedily took the nipple, "and still thinned, but I don't know if it's a good idea to feed you richer food all at once."

She rocked the baby, humming, but then suddenly stopped.

Beans. Beans and pork.

Didn't Sheriff O'Keefe say that Francis Clarke—a man she'd known, although not well, but who had always been pleasant and chipper and willing to lend a hand—had died over a can of beans? One without any meat?

A shudder went though her, unbidden, but then she shook her head.

No, that was just too silly.

Billy sat in his cell, sulking and listening to Slocum tell the sheriff his story. Billy couldn't hear it any too well, since they'd gone back outside, but he could hear most of it plain enough if he listened hard.

Didn't sound too good for him.

He rattled the cell door. It was locked good enough to hold him in, that was for certain.

He tested the bars in the window.

Maybe one of them was a tad loose, but Slocum would have him out of here and on his way to a necktie party before he could begin to get it dug free.

Especially since he didn't have his knife anymore. Slocum had taken that this afternoon, after he'd pulled that fool stunt and tried to ride down on them, shooting.

That was stupid. Asinine! What had made him think that he could catch them by surprise?

Billy had been kicking himself for it ever since he woke and found his head stinging in two places instead of one. It just seemed like he was doomed to get shot in the head, over and over.

Now, what kind of a deal was that?

When he came out of this, he'd have more parts in his hair than any natural man ought to have. *If* he came out of it, that was.

Billy slumped on his cot, letting the murmur of voices turn into a drone in the background. What he needed right now was nothing short of a miracle, and he knew it. He had gone through all the possible escape scenarios he might face on the trail, but this Slocum was no slouch. It seemed he was ready for anything.

If Billy didn't want to find himself dangling from the end of a rope in some two-bit town—and before he'd even had half a chance to make a real name for himself— he'd best start praying right about now.

And curiously enough, that was exactly what he did. He prayed for the hand of God to just stretch in and open his cell, so that he could sink a slug into Slocum's head, not just into his scalp. He prayed for divine intervention so that he might show that Lydia bitch just what was what, goddamn it.

Hell, they'd both tried to kill him! Didn't that justify his killing them?

To his mind, it sure did.

And unbeknownst to him, Billy Cree's prayers were about to be answered. Not in the form that he'd imagined, but it was as close as he was going to get.

High in the rocks, an exhausted Charlie Frame sat, staring down on what had, not too long ago, been the thriving mining town of Cross Point. He had left the bay back a bit, where he wouldn't be poking his head into view in case anybody from the town decided to take a look up this way.

"Well, hell," he mumbled. "I'll be damned. Silver must'a dried up."

He cast a long shadow down the hillside, for the sun was behind him, sinking toward the western horizon. Realizing this, he readjusted his position until not even his shadow was visible.

He figured to wait until dark to go on down. He also figured they wouldn't be expecting him, but that was no reason to go and announce himself by riding down there in broad daylight, or even by casting his shadow down the rise.

Besides, he needed to rest up. He planned on a real exciting night.

As best he could, he settled back into the unforgiving rocks pressing hard against his spine, closed his eyes, and tried to sleep.

"Terrible thing," Sheriff Dusty O'Keefe said through a mouthful of beans and chopped pork. It was a fairly unappetizing sight, although Slocum didn't say anything. If the leprechaun at the end of your rainbow was a toothless old codger who gummed his food and yammered nonstop even while he was gumming it, he was still your leprechaun.

The sheriff swallowed. Thank God. Before he took a fresh bite, he added, "You say them Frame boys kilt the boy's pa, too?"

Slocum helped himself to another biscuit before he said, "That's right. They ought to be trickling down here in a day or so. If I was you, I'd watch my step with 'em."

Sheriff O'Keefe nodded seriously. "I surely will. You folks takin' off in the mornin', then? These is sure mighty good biscuits, Mrs. West. Cain't say as when I've had better."

Slocum had to agree. "Me either, Lydia. They're light as a feather on a canyon breeze."

Lydia blushed, but Slocum couldn't tell if it was because of the compliment. It might have been on account of the bean juice slowing drizzling from the corner of the sheriff's mouth.

Coloring hotly, she looked down at her own plate. "Thank you, gentlemen."

It was the bean drool, then, Slocum figured. He couldn't say that he blamed her.

They were taking their meal in the abandoned Blue Bird Café. Lydia had dusted a table and chairs, baked the biscuits and something for dessert—which smelled to Slocum like a mouthwatering apple cobbler, or maybe a pie— and O'Keefe had volunteered to provide the main meal.

"It'll be beans, you wait and see," Lydia had whispered to Slocum. "If I never see another bean, it'll be too soon."

"It's his town, Lydia," Slocum had replied in his best diplomatic tone.

She had snorted. "Only by default," she'd said, and stalked off into the kitchen.

However, later at the dinner table, she seemed to have forgiven him, for one of her little hands was curled over his thigh. For the third time since sitting down, Slocum willed away his erection and tried to concentrate on his beans.

"Do you get much traffic through here nowadays, Sheriff?" she asked.

Slocum doubted that she cared. She was just trying to make conversation, he supposed.

"Since the silver gave out, you mean, ma'am?" O'Keefe asked. And then without waiting for an answer, he said, "Not so much anymore. Only folks as ain't realized the town's gone to pot. That number gets smaller all the dang time. I was real heartened to see you folks."

"Yes, Sheriff," Lydia said, tearing daintily at a biscuit. "I could tell by the way you were pointing that shotgun at us that you were thrilled at the prospect of our company."

It was O'Keefe's turn to color, and he did: beet-red. A smile flickered over Lydia's mouth before it turned back to the innocent line it had been.

Slocum was just beginning to realize what a fine, dry sense of humor she had.

Still, he figured he really ought to save the sheriff. "Aw now, Lydia honey, the sheriff was just protectin' his town. Any man in his boots would'a done the same."

Lydia stood up and looked first at the sheriff, then Slocum. "Dessert?" she asked innocently.

"Sounds good," Slocum replied.

"Mighty fine!" said O'Keefe. He had scraped his plate clean, and was on his fifth biscuit. "Sure smells like a good apple pie you got cookin' out there, ma'am. Ain't had a pie in a couple'a months of Sundays!"

"I'm afraid it's going to be a few more Sundays, Sheriff O'Keefe," Lydia said as Slocum watched her swish through the swinging door to the kitchen. She reappeared almost instantly, carrying a rectangular baking pan. "It's a cobbler, made with dried apples from the mercantile."

With mitted hands, she slid the pan to the tabletop. "Careful," she said, slipping into her chair again. "It's hot."

"Don't bother me none," O'Keefe said. He was already digging into the cobbler. Slocum dug his spoon in and started heaping cobbler on his plate. He figured that if he didn't hurry, there'd be none left.

And then he remembered Lydia.

As she blinked, he began piling cobbler on her plate with the speed of a man possessed.

"Enough, Slocum!" she said, and put her hand on his.

He grinned at her sheepishly. It was a good thing he'd piled his plate, though, because when he turned back toward the pan, it was empty, and Sheriff O'Keefe's plate was piled a good six inches deep in steaming spiced apples and sweet biscuits.

"Sheriff?" Lydia asked, all innocence.

Slocum, who was nobody's fool, immediately began to tense.

"Ma'am?" O'Keefe asked around a mouthful of half-chewed cobbler.

"You said that Mr. Clarke—Francis—died over a can of beans," she said. "I couldn't help but notice, when I was in the store, that you eat nothing but beans. You didn't shoot Mr. Clarke, did you?"

Slocum thumbed the leather strap off his gun, thinking, *Goddamn it, Lydia! Couldn't you wait until after dessert?*

He'd been thinking about the same thing, but at least he'd the sense to try to fill his belly before he stirred things up.

It seemed Lydia suffered no such inhibitions, though.

She sat there, smiling. "Did you, Sheriff?"

O'Keefe put down his fork and sat back in his chair. "Now, I'm right hurt that you'd ask me that, Mrs. West. Right hurt. As a matter of fact, I did not. I seen it happen, but I didn't do it. Josh Abrams shot him, as sure as I'm sitting here and you folks with me."

Slocum was waiting for somebody to draw. He wasn't entirely certain whether it would be the sheriff or Lydia.

But Lydia's smile never broke. "Thank you, Sheriff. That was all I wanted to know." And when he still sat there, staring at her in disbelief, she added, "Sheriff? Your cobbler's getting cold."

He jerked forward. "Oh! So it is!" he said, and dived back in.

Slocum lifted his hand from below the tabletop and let out a sigh. There were three highly unstable types in the world, and he was sitting here with two of them—old men who had invented their own purpose in life, and women in general.

The first type were wily and tricky and sometimes wise. The second were, well, just women. That was catty-wampus enough and went without further explanation, if you asked him.

Of course, the third type was like Billy Cree or the Frame boys—those cocky, callow boys of all kinds who yearned for a big reputation to see them through life, and figured to make it on Slocum's back.

Slocum comforted himself that Cree was in jail and that the Frame brothers were walking wounded and far back on the trail. And that—for the moment anyway—Lydia's abrupt question had gone surprisingly right and had evaporated every last bit of tension from the room.

He picked up his fork and began working on his cobbler. Lydia sure had a way with baked goods, all right. It was toothsome.

Matter of fact, so was she. He couldn't wait to get supper over with and bed down for the night in some degree of comfort.

And by comfort, he meant Lydia's arms.

20

Night fell.

Charlie Frame roused himself from a light but ragged doze and stood up, stretching as he rose. The rocks had put a few kinks in his back and legs where there hadn't been any before, but an awkward little dance high above the town took care of those.

There were no lights below, but then, he hadn't expected any. Now he was surer than ever that the place was deserted.

"Now, what did you do with Billy Cree?" he whispered. Slocum would have locked him up in the jail, if Charlie was any judge of character.

Yes, that was it. He'd find the jail first and see about Billy. Slocum would be next.

He took a long drink of water, then relieved himself on a jut of rock, sighing deeply as his bladder emptied. Tonight was the night, he reminded himself. Come morning, he'd be a rich man. And he'd have himself a reputation, to boot! Mr. Big-Shot Slocum and Mr. Billy Fancy-Riding Cree, that would be a catch and a half.

Yessir, tonight was the night.

Despite having inspected them before several times, he

thoroughly checked his side arm, then checked his rifle.
They were in good shape and loaded for bear. So to speak.

Grinning broadly, Charlie started back, to get the bay.

Slocum undressed Lydia slowly, relishing the look of her
in the pale, golden lantern light.

There wasn't much undressing to do. She had just
come from an impromptu bath down on the first floor,
and she was only clad in a bathrobe several sizes too big.
Her blond hair, still damp, hung in fairy curls, framing
her face and shoulders, making those long-lashed blue-
green eyes of hers look even bigger, even more vulnera-
ble.

Even more hungry.

He'd had a hard-on more or less since they sat down
to dinner, and now he was about to do something about
it.

Still, he eased the robe from her shoulders slowly, letting it drop and puddle gently on the floor. She didn't
seen ashamed of her nakedness. She merely stood there,
letting him take her all in.

Her breasts were high and firm, her ribs trimming to a
smooth waist and flat little belly, then flaring out gently
into a soft swell of hips. Her legs were long and lean and
almost muscular for a woman. When he brushed his hand
across it, he found the little thatch of hair at the juncture
of her thighs was moist.

She shuddered, and he knew then that the dampness
wasn't left over from any bath. She was as eager as he
was.

Her hands went to the buttons of his shirt and began
to undo them, one by one. He, too, was still a little damp,
having grabbed a quick bath down at the bathhouse while
she was taking hers, here at the hotel.

She opened his shirt and put her face to him, inhaling deeply. "You smell good," she said.

"Likewise," he whispered, and tried to get her to move toward the bed.

But she shrugged off his hand and whispered, "Just hold your horses, Slocum. I want to get a look at you, too."

She was going to get a real big surprise when she got below his belt line.

He stood still.

She pulled the shirttail from his britches and let the sleeves drop down his arm to the floor before she splayed her hands across his chest.

"So wide," she murmured. "So strong." She ran her fingers down one of his scars, an old Apache lance wound that he'd picked up about ten years before.

"So many war wounds, so many battle scars," she went on softly.

"So little time?" he urged. "Lydia? Honey?"

Lightly, she chuckled, and dropped her hands to begin work at his belt buckle.

She had it free in no time, and only excited him further when her hands met his erection. He couldn't help it. The damned thing seemed to have a mind of its own, and fairly leapt out at her.

She fairly purred. "I see what you mean about so little time, Slocum," she said, smiling in the dim lamplight. "Why don't you shuck free of those britches and boots?"

"Ain't gotta ask me twice," he said, kicking them free even as he grabbed her and fell toward the bed. She let out a whoop, laughing, and landed next to him.

He gave a last, freeing kick to his pants and heard a thump as one of his boots hit the opposite wall, then a crash as some of the dusty bric-a-brack hit the floor along with it.

He didn't take the time to look at the damage. He was already too busy with Lydia.

Her arms went around his rib cage as he moved between her legs, his erect cock thumping hungrily against her leg, then at her portal.

He eased his way in with no trouble, and when he did, she let out a long, breathy sigh and lidded her eyes. He stayed still for a moment, kissing her lips, her eyes, her cheeks, her throat and breasts. Her nipples were tight and dark with desire, standing up like two tiny, deep pink thimbles.

When he took one in his mouth and tugged on it playfully with his teeth, Lydia made a sweet little sound in her throat and drew her arms up, around his neck. Her back arched slightly, pushing her breasts toward him.

He began to move.

She rose up to meet him, matching him thrust for thrust. Slowly at first, then with increasing fervor. He escalated the pace at her urging, pacing himself, riding her like a jockey rides a racehorse. He became mindless, losing himself in her erotic timing, her sultry caress, her pumping hips, her heady sighs.

And then that insistent itch in his loins began to quick-burn toward its culmination, like the fuse on blasting powder nearing its goal. He felt it mounting through his veins, pumping toward his groin, sizzling, sizzling.

And then he exploded like fireworks, bigger and better than on the Fourth of July. That best of all-encompassing sensations rocketed out from his groin, enveloped his whole body so that he was certain that the sweet fire would burn him into a cinder.

But then, like always, he came into himself again. He felt himself on the bed, in Lydia's arms, felt the sweat drip from his brow, and heard Lydia's contented sighs beneath him.

He let out a long breath of air and rolled to one side

of her, feeling the sudden rush of cooler air wash over his groin. He slung an arm around her shoulders, then bent to kiss her lips.

Just before he did, she whispered, "Beds are better, Slocum."

"Got to agree with you on that one, darlin'," he whispered back, then kissed her.

Down at the sorry excuse for a town jail, Sheriff O'Keefe was considering whether or not to sweep up the place.

His feet up on the desk, a cup of hot coffee at his side, he surveyed the littered floor and the desk, piled high not with circulars, but with bits of wrapping paper, back issues of the long-departed *Cross Point Express* (the latest issue dated six months back), a couple of rusting horseshoes, his spare shirt, cans long ago emptied of beans or potted pork, spoons crusted with dried food, and an empty whiskey bottle.

He'd drunk that a while back, too.

But now he had something to celebrate. A real prisoner, right here in his jail!

Well, it wasn't exactly *his* jail. It had been Sheriff Turnbull's jail, way back when. Then they had those bandits ride in, looking for a good time, and *boom*, there went Sheriff Turnbull, dead from a slug in his chest.

After that, there wasn't much of anybody left, and then the last few hangers-on filtered out of town. O'Keefe figured that somebody ought to be sheriff. Why not him?

There wasn't much choice about who to elect, was there?

But having a real live prisoner here sort of made it official!

He opened a lower desk drawer and pulled out a brand-new bottle of bourbon, saved from the Swinging Door Saloon, and blew the dust off it. Damned dust got everywhere: inside drawers, on clothes, in cupboards, you name it.

He paused and scowled. Didn't make much sense to clean up when it'd just get all dirty again.

Deciding against cleaning—and feeling like he'd done something, having made the decision not to do anything—he opened the bottle and poured a shot into his coffee.

He had lifted it halfway to his lips when Billy spoke up and half-scared him to death.

"Hey, you! You got any'a that for me?"

O'Keefe curled himself around and took a look at his prisoner. Billy was slouched on his cot, elbows in his knees, his pillaged dinner plate before him on the floor.

O'Keefe didn't answer him. A killer like Billy Cree didn't deserve a reply, to his mind. And a rapist, too! Slocum had told him, and he had to agree that a rapist was the lowest of the low. In O'Keefe's opinion, a man could kill by accident, but he sure as hell didn't accidentally rape somebody.

There was such a thing as the sanctity of womanhood, by God!

He raised his coffee mug to his lips and took a sip. Damn fine stuff, that.

He was smacking his lips when Billy said, "Hey! Didn't you hear me, you damned codger? I said to gimme a drink of that!"

"I heard you just fine, you loathsome piece of trash," O'Keefe said without turning toward him. "Forget it. You ain't gettin' none." He took another sip.

"Listen, you can't just leave a man sittin' in here and drink in front of him when he can't fetch himself a drop," Billy said. "It ain't fair. It ain't even Christian."

But O'Keefe was only half-listening. Was that bootsteps he heard coming up the walk? Mayhap Slocum had decided he wasn't all that tired, and was coming down to keep him company for a spell. He'd like that.

"Shut up," he snapped at Billy. "I told you, no. 'Sides, Slocum's comin'. You want he should be the one to tell you that you can't have any? I guarantee he won't be as polite as me."

That shut Billy up, all right, and O'Keefe smiled. He rummaged around in his deepest drawer for another coffee mug. He thought it was there, anyhow. Been a month of Sundays since anybody was there to use the dang thing.

Just as he put his hand on the mug, the door creaked open, and he looked up expectantly.

Except that the man standing there was a stranger, a beat-up stranger with dried blood on his sleeve and a lot of trail on his britches, who looked back and forth between him and Billy.

"You ain't Slocum," O'Keefe said, and let the mug drop back in the drawer.

From the corner of his eye, he saw Billy smile, which prompted him to reach for his gun.

But it was too late. By the time O'Keefe had gotten his fingers curled around the grip, Charlie Frame had crossed the tiny front room and launched himself over the desk, knocking the coffee to the floor and scattering the mess on the desk and taking a surprised O'Keefe by his narrow throat.

"Hey!" O'Keefe tried to shout, just before everything went dark.

21

Charlie ushered a cackling and eager Billy Cree out the jailhouse door. Charlie was pretty gleeful, too, although he didn't let it show. He was going to let ol' Billy take out Slocum and that lady, and then he was going to take out Billy.

What could be better?

When they gained the street, Billy paused.

"Now, where'd they get to?" Charlie asked him, smooth as glass. Charlie was convinced that he was a very smooth character.

"Hotel," Billy said, checking his gun. "Up the street." He gestured with a tilt of his head.

Charlie stared at the only two-story building on the street. "Don't see no lights."

"So maybe they put up in a room on the other side of the place," Billy said, and rammed his gun back into his holster. "Maybe they ain't got any lights lit." He picked up his rifle and checked it, too.

Charlie waited until he was satisfied with his firearms, then said anxiously, "Well? Let's go!"

Billy nodded, and they started up the street. When they came to the hotel, Billy stopped outside the door.

"What?" demanded Charlie.

"Thinkin'," said Billy.

Charlie wanted this over with, and right now. He didn't want to spend his time standing around and thinking. He wanted some action! Preferably by Billy Cree. And then Charlie would get his taste.

Charlie snorted sharply. He said, "What's there to think about? You just go find 'em and shoot 'em. Done and done."

Billy drew his gun, and for just a second Charlie got pretty nervous. But the gun wasn't for Charlie. Billy pointed it toward the hotel door, then put his hand on the latch.

"Quiet!" he whispered. "Or you can just stay out here."

Charlie didn't want Billy going up there alone. If that was the case, Billy could shoot Slocum and the lady and then do something sneaky, like go out the rear door or a window and sneak back around and plug *him*. No, he wasn't going to take any chances.

His gun arm was still bad, after all. He figured he could put a slug in Billy easy enough, what with Billy trusting him and all. But he needed Billy to kill Slocum and whatshername so that he could get his hands on the kid— and the mine—and he needed Billy to believe that he was on the right side.

Meaning Billy's.

"Oh, don't worry. I'll be quiet as a church mouse," Charlie whispered, nodding. "Now, go on. I got your back."

Not that he had any such intention . . .

Upstairs, Slocum was sitting up in bed, rolling himself a quirlie. Beside him, Lydia lounged against the pillows, happy as a cat with her belly full of cream. The night had been pretty eventful so far, and she figured it was only going to get more interesting.

She had found food for the baby, rocked him to sleep, had a bath, and gotten herself laid by probably the best gunslinger she'd ever had the pleasure to meet. She let out a long, contented sigh. He looked like he could go all night, too.

That sordid business with Billy Cree and his boys was shoved into the dark recesses of her mind, along with all the bad things that had happened to her during her checkered life. It hadn't been the worst. Of course, it sure hadn't been the best either. Winston West she had already mourned. Dear old Winston, who had taken her out of that whorehouse and brought her into decent society as his wife.

She had been angry with Winston for a while, there. Angry because he hadn't told her about his former life, and angry because, well, he'd died. He'd saved her life, then left her to dangle in the wind, so to speak.

But he couldn't help it, could he? He couldn't help Billy Cree and his thugs riding down and bushwhacking him right there in the front yard.

Of course, he could have told her about it in the first place. And he could have told her that he was already married, the rat . . .

She let it go. Winston was dead and gone and wouldn't be coming back. She'd always be grateful to him, but her life wasn't over.

She had a baby to raise. Or try to raise. Try to talk somebody into letting her raise him, more like.

Well, she'd do it. She had lived through the last week, hadn't she? To her mind, if she could do that, she could do just about anything.

And Slocum? He wasn't the staying kind. She'd known that the moment she first laid eyes on him. By my goodness, he had certainly come in handy. Saved her life, for one thing. She'd never have made it to town. If she hadn't died of exposure first, Billy Cree—couldn't that sonofabitch stay dead, for heaven's sake?—would have tracked her down and killed her.

And little Tyler never would have come to her.

She had grown incredibly fond of that baby. She'd never thought she had the stuff in her to be a mother, but the first moment that Slocum had placed him in her arms . . . She supposed she'd known from the start. He was meant to be hers.

"Penny for your thoughts?" Slocum said. He had just lit his smoke. He offered it to her.

Smiling, she shook her head no. "I was just thinking. About you, and the baby, and that sorry louse Billy Cree."

But he didn't appear to be listening. To her anyway. He was staring at the door, his brow wrinkled.

"Slocum?" she whispered.

And then she saw it—the knob, slowly turning. "Is it O'Keefe?" she whispered, even though she knew it wasn't. He would have knocked.

A sudden surge of adrenaline coursed through her veins.

Slocum was already up and reaching for his guns. She didn't need anybody to tell her what to do. Stark naked, she quickly rolled off the bed to the floor, and silently scuttled into a far corner.

Lydia was smart. He hadn't had to tell her a thing, and already she was over in the corner, tucked behind the bureau and hugging her knees. And she'd had the sense— or the accidentally good graces—to throw the covers back up, so that it looked like somebody could still be sleeping there.

He had gone across the room, toward the door, and now waited in back of it, his back against the wall. He stood there, barely breathing, gun in hand, as the door slowly creaked open.

The first thing he saw was a hand, gripped to a pearl-handled Colt.

He knew that gun. It was Billy Cree's.

Operating on reflex alone, he brought his pistol down hard, smack on Billy's wrist.

Billy yelped and dropped the gun even as Slocum grabbed his arm and slung him across the floor. He heard boots running down the hall and down the stairs, as Billy skidded into the far wall.

Who did he have out there, helping him? He didn't figure old O'Keefe could run that fast.

"Get up," he growled.

"Goddamn it! You busted my wrist!" Billy howled, holding it close to his chest.

"Who was out there with you?" Slocum demanded.

Billy, in obvious agony, snarled, "Nobody! Go to hell!" Then he took a closer look. "You're bare naked!"

Slocum rolled his eyes.

Lydia was already on her feet and wrapping herself in a sheet. "Give me that," she said, holding out her hand. "I can cover this sonofabitch while you dress."

Slocum handed over the gun without comment. He quickly pulled on his britches and gunbelt, shoved his boots on over his feet, and slithered into his shirt. Tucking in his shirttail, he started for the door.

"Just don't kill him till I get back," he growled, and slipped out into the hall. "Shoot first and ask questions later if anybody—and I mean anybody—tries to open this door. Unless it's me."

"Right," she said, casting as evil a smile as he was likely to see down at Billy Cree.

Quietly closing the door behind him, Slocum pulled the gun from his left holster, shifted it to his right hand, and started stealthily down the hallway.

●　●　●

Panting, Charlie ducked around the corner of the building, his gun in his trembling hand.

"Get hold of yourself, boy," he muttered, "get hold!"

He was in for it now. How had Slocum seen them coming, anyhow? They been tiptoeing out there in the hall. They'd heard Slocum and the lady talking. He was sure that they hadn't been on the alert.

But then, when Billy opened the door, there was Slocum, the sonofabitch. Why, the man must be a mystic or a witch or something! It was the only thing Charlie could figure.

And now Slocum would be coming after him.

Great, just great.

He stilled himself long enough to take a long listen to the hotel at his back. There was nothing. No sound, not even Billy yelping about his goddamn hand. Some people could sure be babies about their wounds. Not Charlie. Charlie was what you call stoic. Brave and silent, that was his code.

Goddamn it.

But how was he supposed to kill Slocum when his gun arm was stove up? *Thanks,* he added mentally, *to that bastard, Slocum.*

"No, it was the woman," he reminded himself in a whisper. "Now, just calm the hell down. Ice, boy. You're ice."

And strangely enough, his blood seemed to chill and his heart seemed to slow from the pounding thing it had been in his chest.

"All right, Slocum," he whispered. "You're gonna meet your maker at the hands of Charlie Frame, sure as I'm standin' here."

A smile started to snake across his lips, but before it was halfway there, a gun cocked. Right next to his ear.

He froze, and slowly, his eyes swiveled in their sockets to the left.

Sonofabitch!

• • •

"Ouch, boy! Careful, there!"

"O'Keefe, you gotta be more careful about who you let in this place," Slocum said.

Lydia, who was treating O'Keefe's bruised neck, said, "Now Slocum, how could he expect that Charlie would show up?"

"That's the whole deal," Slocum said, frowning at Billy Cree and Charlie Frame, who now resided in Billy's old cell. They regarded each other angrily from opposite cots. "You got to be ready for the unexpected. All the time."

Charlie snorted, and Slocum added, "You boys just go on ahead and kill each other, all right? It'll save a jury the trouble of hangin' you."

"Yes, Charlie," piped up Lydia. "Please go on ahead and kill Billy Cree. Pay you ten dollars for it."

"Ten lousy dollars?" Billy, holding his hand, shouted. "That's an insult!"

"I meant it to be," Lydia cooed.

"Now, kiddies," Slocum muttered. "Play nice."

"I'm fixed, I tell you," said Sheriff O'Keefe and pulled away from Lydia. "Gosh darn it, lady, I think you're bloodthirsty."

Lydia dusted her hands. "Isn't any more I can do, anyway. You're already starting to color up, Sheriff. You're going to have yourself quite a bruise in the morning."

"And no folks around to admire it," O'Keefe said, shaking his head. "Life sure ain't fair."

"If you only knew what you threw away with being so blamed noisy," Charlie muttered nastily to Billy. "You'd just kill yourself and get it over with."

"Shut up before I crown you," spat Billy.

"Like you could," said Charlie. "You crummy two-bit outlaw. What'd you ever do 'cept rob a few stages and a bank, anyhow?"

Billy leaned forward. "It's more than you've done, you hick!"

"That's right, boys," Slocum said as he took Lydia's arm. By the clock on the wall, it was after ten. Time for him to be in bed. With Lydia.

"Just keep it up," he added. "I'd be obliged."

"Me, too," Lydia said as he drew her out the door.

"Shut up, bitch!" shouted Billy Cree.

"Night, O'Keefe," Slocum said, and closed the door behind them.

"I can't say I'm looking forward to traveling with those two," Lydia said with a shake of her head.

"Don't worry about it," Slocum replied. "I'll send somebody back for 'em, when we get to Apache Wells. Talked to O'Keefe about it, earlier. He'll hold on to those boys for a few days, until a marshal can come and fetch 'em."

"That's the nearest town?" she said. "Apache Wells?"

He nodded.

"I wonder what happened to the other one. Ed."

"Still back there, according to Charlie," Slocum said. He's walkin' in, like a good boy."

"How did Charlie get to town so fast, anyway?"

Slocum shrugged. "Easy," he said. "He ran most of the way. And I guess that just before Billy came riding down on us like a house a-fire, he'd abandoned a spare horse. Charlie picked it up."

Lydia hugged his arm. She shook her head. "He's absolutely crazy, isn't he?"

Slocum chuckled. "Wouldn't be a bit surprised, honey."

They came to the hotel, and stepped up on the walk. Slocum put his hand over hers and turned toward her. "Now, what you say we don't talk about those two anymore? Let's take advantage of this night, and that nice mattress upstairs."

She grinned up at him, her eyes and moist lips glinting softly in the moonlight. "Sounds fine to me, Slocum. How long will it take us to get to Apache Wells, anyway?"

Slocum opened the door and held it for her. "Couple of days."

She passed through. "Will O'Keefe be all right? I mean, with Ed coming and all?"

Slocum lit a candle. He said, "You met the same Ed that I did?"

She cocked her head to the side, then grinned just a little. "You're right. O'Keefe will be fine. Two days on the trail, you said?"

They started up the stairs.

"Yes, ma'am," he replied, thinking about the nights more than the days.

And she was, too, because she said, "Then we'd best take advantage of this mattress while we have it, hadn't we?"

22

By the time Ed Frame dragged himself into Cross Point, Slocum and Lydia and the baby were long gone, and he found himself greeted by the nose of Sheriff Dusty O'Keefe's trusty Greener.

"You Ed Frame?" the sheriff asked, after he'd introduced himself and relieved Ed of his side arm and rifle.

"Maybe," Ed replied wittily.

"Right," the sheriff said, and jabbed the shotgun's nose into Ed's belly. "I knowed it was you the second you come limpin' in here with that game leg. It gangrened yet?"

"Don't think so," Ed replied with a gulp. Frankly, he hadn't thought to check. But it didn't smell funny, which gave him hope.

"All right, then." Another jab with the shotgun. "Turn around and march on down the street. When you see the jail, turn in."

"But I never done nothin'!" Ed complained. "Never in Cross Point, leastwise."

"That's true," said the sheriff with a curt nod. "You ain't. But still, I got to hold you till somebody gets this mess sorted out. Now, march. Your brother's waitin' for you."

Ed started moving, but he asked, "You mean a skinny old coot like you got my brother?"

"And Billy Cree, too," the sheriff announced proudly. "Slocum helped me some, I reckon. He's one heck of a fella, that Slocum."

Slocum and Lydia pulled into Apache Wells a day later, and Slocum, after a long talk with the judge, managed to arrange Lydia's adoption of "Unnamed Tyler".

"I suppose he ought to have a first name," Lydia said back at the hotel after a celebration bout of lovemaking.

Slocum jammed an extra pillow behind his head and rested one hand on the generous pillow of Lydia's breast. "What, then? I reckon you can name him Justin, after his pa."

"Maybe. Or after his savior. You have a first name, Slocum?"

"John."

"John Tyler," she said, considering. "John Justin Tyler. I like that."

"Sounds fine." He was looking at Lydia's hair. It was spread out over the pillows like a great golden fan, and sparkled in the sunlight that peeked through the curtains. "You decide about where you're goin'?"

"East or west, you mean?" She pursed her lips.

He nodded.

"West," she said. "I think west. There's nothing for me back east. That was just a dream I had, when I knew I couldn't have it. You know what I mean?"

Slocum supposed he did, and grunted in the affirmative. He wanted to bury his face in that hair of hers. Or maybe dive headlong into those great big blue-green eyes. It was a dilemma.

"So I suppose I'll take him—baby John, that is," she

added with a smile, "out to California. It was where his folks were taking him, after all. Maybe somebody there knew his uncle. And besides," she added, "I have to look out for his interests, now."

Slocum was only half-listening. He lowered his head and lapped at her nipple, then took it into his mouth.

She put her hand behind his head, cupping it, and softy said, "You didn't hear a word I said, did you?"

He lifted his lips long enough to say, "Sure. California." He got back to business.

Lydia squirmed and made a little purring sound, down in her throat. "Some men just have a one-track mind," she whispered, and slid her hand down his chest, toward his crotch.

"Some ladies, too," he said, chuckling, around her nipple.

"Oh, there are no ladies here, Slocum," she said, lifting his chin.

Smiling, she kissed him.

Watch for

SLOCUM AND THE LADY REPORTER

304th novel in the exciting SLOCUM series
from Jove

Coming in June!

Explore the exciting Old West with one of the men who made it wild!

J. R. ROBERTS

THE GUNSMITH